Tales of Eve

edited by Mhairi Simpson

F♦X SPIRIT

www.foxspirit.co.uk

'Tales of Eve' edited by Mhairi Simpson

Cover Art by Daniele Serra
http://www.multigrade.it/

typesetting and ebook conversion by handebooks.co.uk

ISBN: 978-1-909348-19-6 mobi
978-1-909348-20-2 epub
978-1-909348-21-9 pb

A Fox Spirit Original
Fox Spirit Books
www.foxspirit.co.uk
adele@foxspirit.co.uk

Never underestimate a woman

Contents

Introduction

Mhairi Simpson

Writing, for me, is long periods of isolation punctuated with rather random conversations. The conversations usually occur in the presence of both food and alcohol and have ways of unlocking parts of my brain I didn't know I had until they stepped out, stretching their fingers and toes, tilting their faces towards the sun, before turning to me and saying, "Now then…"

The conversation which led to this collection occurred over dinner at alt.fiction 2012, and the idea was simple: the annals of story are filled with men creating the perfect woman, but what about women creating the perfect man?

Over the next couple of months this expanded to women creating the perfect partner, and although I originally intended someone else to edit it, I eventually gave up on finding anyone to do the job, and the results lie spread across the following pages.

The beauty of this particular great idea, of course, is that I didn't have to write it. I got a bunch of rather talented other people to do that for me. And, my, have they done a fine job!

From Adrian Tchaikovsky's horribly skilled artificers to Ren Warom's desperate companion, this is a collection of stories highlighting the ingenuity of the female mind. But not just that. They also show the lengths women will go to, be it for loneliness, love, or even science, to achieve their goals.

It has been my very great pleasure (and sometimes spine-weakening terror) to edit these stories, bringing together a diverse mix of published and unpublished authors in a variety of takes on the theme. I'm particularly honoured to play host to Juliet McKenna's sci-fi debut, *Game, Set and Match?* and Paul Weimer's worldwide debut, *Newton's Method*.

Newton's Method actually kicks off the collection with a

woman so determined to find a partner that she creates much more than a mere machine. I was particularly entertained by the demonstration of how people become more choosy when provided with options. Weimer has done a brilliant job here and I look forward to reading more of his work in the future.

Ellie Danger, Girl Daredevil raised hairs on the back of my neck, and I sincerely hope Alasdair Stuart writes more in this world. The idea that you are often the only person you can rely on is dealt with beautifully here and as such the story lingers in your mind long after you finish reading it.

Father's Day was another unique take on the theme - who would be a child's perfect companion? Francesca Terminiello puts together a heartwarming story about the consequences of single parenthood, and a different kind of magic.

The CompaniSIM, The Treasure, The Thief And Her Sister takes the reader into a virtual world, and I love that all the main characters in this story are female. Not because I'm against male characters, but because each plays a part in the creation of one or more of the others as the tale unfolds. Paget's skill in blending these with a high tech world produces a fascinating story.

Andrew Reid's *Kate and the Buchanan* presents a whole new perspective on the possibilities afforded by machinery. I was almost moved to violence at one point when someone I thought deserved it did not, in fact, get hit over the head with a wrench. But Reid more than makes up for that in the end.

Game, Set and Match? represents Juliet McKenna's science fiction debut, and inspired the most editorial comments along the lines of "Aha! Take that!" in the margins. It represents a triumph for feminism, in its true sense, and leaves the reader with a sense of hope and happiness.

In Memoriam, on the other hand, almost made me cry several times. Rob Haines' depiction of artificial intelligence gave me shivers, and still does. It also made me look up at the sky, wondering what may or may not be out there.

I'm not sure I'm supposed to admit to this, but *Unravel* is my personal favourite. Where *In Memoriam* almost made me cry, *Unravel* made me sob unashamedly for hours, which did slow the editorial process somewhat. Ren Warom has combined desperation, love, determination and sheer ingenuity in a protagonist you will not soon forget.

Mother Knows Best had me laughing out loud, which I think is what the reader needs after *Unravel*. Suzanne McLeod's magical story of one woman trying to live her life while dealing with motherly machinations is brilliantly entertaining and I'm sure most readers, of either gender, will be able to relate.

Adrian Tchaikovsky's *Fragile Creation* scared me to shaking point, and ends the collection with a powerful warning not to underestimate the female of the species. Any species.

The best thing about editing this anthology wasn't that I got to see every story before anyone else (although that came very close), or that I got to see so many wonderful tales from so many talented authors (although that too was brilliant). It's that I know these people at all. Between Adele Wearing (Feral Leader at Fox Spirit) and various conventions, I have been fortunate enough to encounter a number of people who are as ridiculously talented as they are unfailingly supportive. I consider myself honoured that so many of them were able to contribute to this collection, and I hope you enjoy their tales of the female spirit as much as I did.

Mhairi Simpson
Westgate-on-Sea
March 2013

Newton's Method

Paul Weimer

'At last,' she whispered, as she looked over her handiwork. The house gave silent answer, as it had for far too long. Truth be told, she had finished an hour ago, but then she had taken a long shower to wash away the grease, sweat, and tension she'd felt at completing her invention. She was eager to test it out, of course, but she forced herself to relax, to wind down, and to think about what she had built. Years of practical mechanical engineering learned at her mother's knee, combined with the theoretical physics of her father's work, had come to fruition.

Is it selfish of me? Noys thought, *to use this for such a personal purpose?* She shook her head, denying the thought. She wasn't changing the world with her device, just the world she was in.

Noys regarded the front display. She could have used digital readouts and touch screen inputs, making it look more 21st century than 20th century retropunk. Steve Jobs instead of IBM. But the red segmented numbers on the display, reminiscent of an ancient calculator, and the white dials to set parameters, gave it charm and a very tactile note. *Mother would approve*, Noys thought. She felt a pang in her chest at the memory of the drunken driver who took both of her parents on that icy January night.

Noys took a deep breath, and started turning the three dials. Three dials to change the three dimensional axes of what Frederick K. Newton's physics called the three post quaternary dimensions. *Thanks, Dad,* she thought. She fought down the indelible memory of the phone call from the hospital, asking her to come. The sorrowful tone of voice from the grief counsellor, telling what she already instinctively knew in her heart. Instead, she focused on what her parents had taught her. A modest change first. Even a small one. Surely, she wasn't as unsocialized as she thought, and a close branch of her own world would have what she was seeking.

The soft hum of the machine only increased slightly, cycling like a washing machine heard at a distance. Did she make a mistake in the calculations? she wondered, nibbling her lip. Did she need to stand closer to the machine? She thought she had set the field to a 2 meter radius, but what if a mistake in the calculations made that a 20 centimetre radius? With the machine attuned to her, it would only take itself, and her, to the new universe. But she had to be within its range.

Had anything happened at all? Noys stared at the red numerals on the display. Wu +3. Yin -2. Zeta +1. All as measured from Homeline.

They suggested she had made a successful transition. She didn't feel different, though. She closed her eyes and breathed in the air. Was that the smell of ham? And she thought she heard something beyond the machine. Or was this all her imagination? She remained where she stood, not yet daring to leave her machine without further evidence that something had happened.

Noys was relieved when the soft white noise of the machine was momentarily drowned out by a voice.

'Sweetie!' A man's voice. From a nearby room. 'Stop messing with that. Breakfast is ready. Your favorite!' That scent she thought she had smelled finally registered in her nostrils. Sausage? Bacon? No, she really had smelled ham!

Her heart hammered in her chest. *It worked! It worked!* She had changed worlds, and found one where her shyness had not kept her from finding a man. She closed her hands into fists, nails digging into her palms, an old nervous habit.

'I can do this. I can do this,' she said softly. This was what she wanted, what she was looking for. What she needed. She turned around the room in a circle. Was it her imagination, or did it look shabbier? The bookcases were pine, not teak, and fewer books were on them. A long dark stain marred the pale rug, evidence of some long-ago spill.

There are going to be other changes, she thought. It was even possible her parents... She stopped the thought. Whatever the other changes would be, she could live with them. She skipped out of her office and into and through her bedroom. A bigger bed! It was a tangle of sheets rather than crisply made. But Noys didn't care. She could live with that. Besides, it might imply that she'd had no time to make the bed this morning, she thought breathlessly.

In the kitchen, manning the stove, a basic gas stove rather than the high-tech electric stove she knew, was a short man with a tangle of hair. What was left of it anyway. He wore a dingy white wife beater and shorts that didn't cover much of his hairy legs.

'Sweetie!' he said, turning to look at Noys. Noys stopped in her tracks. He didn't seem to read her suddenly stiff body language. He gave a snaggle-toothed grin. 'Ham is ready,' he said, sounding pleased. 'Eggs will be next.'

'I can fix this,' she muttered.

'I'll be right back, honey. I need... I need to, err, brush my teeth,' she said. She fled back to the computer room. For good measure, she closed the door behind her, took a deep breath, and faced the device.

'That was just a first attempt,' she said to herself. 'It was an approximation to the root of the equation.' She could take this result and use it to converge on a better root. Of course she wouldn't get it right on the first try. It was foolish of her to think she would! But a second one...

She reached for the dials, and turned them again. A little more Wu, a little less Zeta. Keep Yin the same. Focus in on the solution. Activate the machine.

Again, there was no sensation of movement that she could tell.

'Honey?' a voice came, muffled by the door. Which was now solid steel? 'Um, I'm hungry. Breakfast? Please?'

Noys opened the door. It sounded like it was pressurized.

A blond haired man lounged on a round (round?!) bed whose pale white sheets contrasted against his sooty-dark skin and dark eyes. She smiled into those dark eyes. And then her appraisal of the rest of him made her think that he would do. Her heart started that hammer beat again.

'I know you're a big time physicist and got plenty of work to do,' the man said, lounging back, lowering his hand to his stomach. Noys' eyes followed, and saw that below that, he wasn't wearing much. As opposed to the nothing above it. 'But Papa needs some breakfast. Oh, and the dry cleaning needs to be picked up. And we're out of milk.'

Noys blinked in surprise. 'Well, we could split the chores,' she found herself saying. *Was the version of her in this world a complete pushover?* Or, did she create a man who thought she was? What did this guy actually do for a living? She hoped he liked bagels; she wasn't much of a cook. At least Snagglepuss had cooked. It had been the only appealing thing about him.

'Sweetie?' the man said. His eyebrows furrowed. 'What are you talking about? The store is three miles away, and the dry cleaning is even further. You don't want me to get picked up by one of the Hippo gangs for being out without a woman to protect me, do you? Probably wind up with some pencil-thin Exasis user who'll slap me around for kicks when she's coming off her highs.' His pupils dilated and he drew a sharp breath. 'Is this your way of trying to get rid of me?'

'I can fix this,' Noys whispered to herself, like a prayer. She fled to the computer room and was relieved that the steel door kept the man's pleas at bay. She repeated her mantra again and again as she returned to the dials.

She kept searching and refining. Through twenty-six distinct attempts.

John Cross seemed nice enough, but the apartment building they lived in sounded like it was in a free-fire zone. The telepaper warning about rebel forces moving south through New Aalborg was enough to send Noys back to the computer room.

Corwin Olson was charming, tall (so very tall), and handsome. But he smoked, and worse, seemed to think he was the center of the universe. He was a single dad, although his son Merlin (*where DID they get the names in this world?*) was now an adult, and according to Corwin, was being driven crazy by his mother, who Corwin tried to avoid as much as possible. 'The Queen Mother,' he called her, although Noys got the impression his ex was younger than he, not older. Noys wondered, if Corwin was arrogant and self-centred, how much worse could Dara really be?

One iteration had Noys wind up in a world where she was indeed married—not to a man, but to Alise Wells, a photographer and artist. Noys had apparently given up her family name for Alise, and was no longer a Newton.

That was surprising. Alise was sweet and caring, and extremely confused by Noys' standoffishness. She seemed to expect a very demonstrative relationship. But Noys was not interested in a relationship with another woman.

Noys started to wonder at the efficacy of her method. A slight change in just one dial was enough to change things, sometimes radically. On one world, she'd been dead for two years and the house was abandoned. She had been married, but seeking out her widower was too creepy by half, even if she pretended to be someone else like in Vertigo, that Hitchcock movie. *That movie ended tragically, too,* she thought.

But with only a slight change in Zeta, and the other settings kept the same, she found a world where her husband had recently died of something horrible the newspaper called Soderbergh-Nine. It was a pandemic spreading across the globe, fast, and there seemed to be no cure. The wrong bat had met the wrong pig, and the result was decimating humanity. Was she immune to this disease? Had she created a world where she was immune? There were locks on every window. The front door had three.

Would a radical change of the dials lead to worlds where her equipment wouldn't be able to recharge, or worse, there was no technology besides it? She imagined the machine sending her on a one way trip to a universe where she was wife or concubine to one of the sons of the Great Khan, living in a yurt. A more portable machine, or perhaps one that doubled as a vehicle, were the next obvious iterations. Once she found what she was looking for and could keep him.

Several were misses for other reasons. What good was a relationship with Michael Lawrence if he was away on a business trip to Albion (Australia, Noys figured out, from a map) for the next six months? Cameron Isley came by the night after Noys activated the device, but apparently it was to get his stuff. Noys still wasn't sure who had instigated his departure.

That experience did get her to thinking, albeit briefly, about the lives she was inhabiting. Were they ever changed by her passing through them? But did they really even exist until Noys activated her machine? Was she finding worlds, or creating them? And how could she tell the difference? She finally decided she was creating both worlds and men in her quest to fill that aching hole in her heart. It might have been simpler to try and find a world where her parents were alive, but that wouldn't have been healthy. She needed a man, a family of her own. Then she would be happy. Then she wouldn't be so very alone, as she had been for the last three years.

Finally, on the twenty seventh try, she hit gold. With Hadrian.

Hadrian D. Macduff was an ex-pat from Greater Scotland who worked as a calculor carder. *A computer programmer,* Noys figured out. He worked for a firm involved with space launch projects. He loved hiking in the mountains, experimenting with Tongan cuisine, and thought The Stones of Tara, a fantasy movie about a pair of sisters drawn into intrigue in a Celtic themed otherworld, was the greatest movie ever made. He apparently not only owned a kilt, but knew how to put it on. And he looked good in one, judging from the pictures of them together.

And Noys could sink into those blue eyes of his and be lost forever.

After a long conversation over dinner (shredded pork wrapped in taro and banana leaves) Hadrian carried her off to bed, although it was really more a case of each of them dragging the other.

Noys sat up in the bed and watched the news on the flat panel screen as the dark haired man beside her slept soundly. Early dawn light filtered into the bedroom. He didn't even snore, she thought. And her core still tingled from the night before. He was so very attentive and passionate.

Those fond memories melted away as she watched the news. There was nothing else. No baseball games. The Olympics had been cancelled. A naval shooting war between the Kingdom of Hawaii and the Tongan Confederacy had apparently stopped of its own accord. Even the weather report was delivered in a manner that was perfunctory at best. The vast majority of the newscast was all about the same thing. Every newscast on every channel was. The sepulchral tones of the talking heads caused Noys to shiver uncontrollably.

Six days. Six days left until Hareb-Sarep hit Earth. Scientists calculated it would likely hit somewhere in the Pacific basin (here called the Lemurian Ocean). Global cooling, already an issue in this world, would accelerate into a full blown ice age, and the tsunamis and earthquakes following the projected strike suggested the death toll would be in the 8 or even 9 figure range.

Los Santos, what they called a city covering the majority of what she knew as the Los Angeles basin, would likely be wiped off the face of the earth. And where could Noys and Hadrian go to escape? The Unified Dominions were roomy, to be sure, but life anywhere in the world after impact would be nasty, brutish and likely short.

No wonder, Noys thought, *Hadrian was confused over dinner.* Perhaps he thought her in denial. But even so, he had treated her with such kindness that she could believe the version of Noys here had been handfasted (their version of marriage) to Hadrian for six years already. And to hear him wax rhapsodic about anything and everything made her soul sing. He was the man with whom she could make the family she desperately craved.

But what price the perfect mate, if the world was for

naught? The machine was created by her, tuned to her. She couldn't take Hadrian. She could probably re-attune it to send Hadrian from this world, and leave herself behind before the end. She expected that he would not even accept such a Faustian bargain, were she despondent enough to offer it to him.

Six days wasn't nearly enough to redesign the machine to take both of them. She wasn't even sure it was theoretically possible. She probably created this world, and thus created him, with a unique resonance not her own. They might well be sent off to completely different destinations without major adjustments to the machine.

There was not enough time to research the problem. Even if she headed back to Homeline to do the work, the underlying theory predicted that time marched forward equally in all of these worlds. She didn't have enough to save herself and Hadrian.

Not enough time by far. There was only one option left.

I can fix this, she thought, sadly, as she got carefully out of their bed and crept to the computer room.

Ellie Danger, Girl Daredevil

Alasdair Stuart

Ellie Danger had gravity. She stood, arms folded, the oversized flight jacket that was her trademark bulking out every inch of her 17-year old frame, and watched a priest who had never met her mentor babble through a eulogy that sounded like he was reading it off cards. He was the best man for the job, the Grief and Recovery Team had assured her. Quantum had left her the labs and the mansion in his will, she knew that much, but there was no word on anything that mattered, not the plane, or the robots, or the other house, the one where the fun stuff was kept. The Dee Institute could grab all the toys it wanted, even from there, but if they touched the plane? Things would get dangerous.

Ellie scowled, watched the priest race the storm, and tried once again to keep her temper in check. Clouds had been building above Elysian Island for the last ten minutes and the priest had got steadily faster as Ellie hunkered lower in her flight jacket, glowering at him. Every one of the committee members had made their apologies, whether in person or in writing, but they'd all, somehow, found a reason to not turn up to the funeral. They'd ignored Professor Niles Quantum whilst he was alive, so it only made sense they'd ignore him now he was dead. It didn't help, it didn't bring her any comfort at all or make her any more sympathetic towards the priest, but she could understand it.

He stumbled over the final few lines and she almost

snapped, almost went for him. What stopped her was the image of Niles Quantum's precise, fox-like nose twitching slightly, his head shaking in a small but definitive 'no.' She swore under her breath, shoved her hands up into the flight jacket he had given her and tried very hard to think about something other than punching a priest in the face.

Finally, he stopped talking, sagging with relief, and the coffin was lowered into the ground. It was cardboard, just like Quantum had wanted. He'd always insisted on keeping his experiments as ecologically friendly as possible and had drawn up strict instructions in his will that his body be placed in a bio-degradable container. He'd made a joke about compost and she'd laughed politely, and then they'd had tea.

And then he'd died.

The priest, looking like he was late for an appointment, muttered hurried, awkward condolences to her and set off back towards the chapel. She turned away when she saw him break into a jog.

Ellie closed her eyes, bit the inside of her cheek as hard as she could and refused to cry. She took a deep breath, looked up at the storm clouds, then turned and headed back towards the airfield. If she was lucky, she could get airborne and out of the area before the storm really hit.

As she turned to go, the storm clouds began to accelerate, roiling and turning over one another until, suddenly, the rain broke over the northern end of the island, a great curtain of water that obscured everything behind it. Everything except a tall woman in her late-30s, her long red hair tied back in a loose ponytail. She was dry, despite the rain, and she moved cautiously but definitively, picking her way through the tombs until she found the grave Ellie had just left. She stood and watched the Nants replace the soil, a stream of golden points that glowed as they patiently moved every grain of soil back to its original position. She didn't cry, she didn't let her eyes close. She didn't blink. Then, without looking up, she spoke.

'You must be soaked.'

She was dressed in good boots, a dark red leather trench

coat with a white tunic underneath it, and had a pen stuck behind her ear, long loops of red hair breaking free of her ponytail and framing her face. Ellie could see the symbol of the Institute seared onto the coat's left breast; an Ouroborous. Knowledge without end. The woman smiled crookedly, looking across at Ellie and speaking with an accentless voice. 'I'm sorry, I wanted to wait until the mourners had gone. I was trying to be discreet. I thought the rain would cover my ClockGate opening.'

Ellie nodded, still unsure of herself and refusing to show it.

'The Institute likes to schedule rain for funerals, helps with the mood. The lightning?' Ellie raised a hand, waggled it from side to side. 'Little bit much after the third strike. Time traveller, right?'

The woman smiled broadly, the loose strands of hair by her ear already plastered down by the storm. 'Well done. I'm Professor Tachyon. You can call me Lucy.'

'You didn't answer my question.'

'Yes, I'm a time traveller. Call me Lucy.'

Ellie folded her arms, part of her revelling in the way the bulky flight jacket made her look bigger than she was. 'I was always told not to speak to strange time travellers.'

Lucy laughed, and sat down against the tomb across from Quantum's. It read:

MATTHEW CHANCE, GENIUS OF NO FIXED
ABODE
BINGO, FAITHFUL COMPANION TO THE END
THEIR ABODE IS FIXED, AND THEY HAVE COME
HOME

Lucy drew a leg up under herself, ignoring the damp, and nodded approvingly. 'Good girl. Niles taught you never to take anything at face value.'

'He was Professor Quantum. Now what do you want? A quick gawp at the last hero of Edinburgh's funeral?'

Lucy smiled. 'Oh, he's not the last. No, I actually came to take a look at this place.' She looked around at the island, at the rows of graves and tombs extending for miles in every direction. The rain had passed over them and Ellie could see it working its way down the island. She hoped it caught the priest before he got inside.

Lucy nodded down the island, towards the dock. 'Did you know the Dee Institute bought it from the crown? Dee himself said that science demanded sacrifice and those who were sacrificed should have somewhere of their own. An Elysium of geniuses. A necropolis of the New Renaissance. In my time, the entire Wyngard section, over there? Covered in genetically engineered hallucinogenic flowers. The old bugger turned his entire family into seed beds for a gentle, psychotropic high. Ninety nine percent of the people who experience it say they meet their loved ones on a hilltop over-looking countryside like nowhere on Earth. They think it might be heaven.'

Ellie swallowed hard, trying and failing not to think about asking if Lucy had the drug with her. 'Why are you here?'

Lucy didn't answer her, instead walking forward and brushing a hand over Quantum's gravestone, also made of cardboard. There was a small blue spark as she did so. When she looked at Ellie again, her face was completely serious and utterly composed. Her voice, when she spoke, was cracked and hoarse. 'Because in my time this cemetery is so much bigger. They had to move the heliport out to sea to make—' Her voice caught and she looked away.

Ellie steeled herself, in that way Quantum had remarked she always did when she was about to do something stupid, then walked over to the other woman, winced slightly and placed a hand on her shoulder. There was a *SNAP!* and the cooking smell of tachyons and heated leather rose from her gloved hand. The woman whipped round, looking at her shoulder, then at Ellie, who was grinning widely, looking at her hand. *Dangerous.*

'You could have killed us!' The older woman spoke with-out thinking and stopped short. Suddenly her right hand half rose to her mouth, realisation flushing her face.

Gotcha, Ellie thought.

After a moment, Lucy composed herself and smiled. 'That was very dangerous, you know.'

Ellie inclined her head, conceding the point. 'Ellie Danger, Girl Daredevil. Localised electrostatic discharge caused when the same matter at different times is somehow brought together.' This time when she spoke it was that voice Quantum had used whenever he was dealing with someone who could be a threat, chatty but iron hard just below the surface. 'Why exactly do I change my name?'

Lucy opened her mouth, closed it, struggled for words.

Ellie spoke, not unkindly. 'You choose this day and this spot and this time to visit a grave that's still there in your time? I don't think so. You're in better shape than I am, but you're older, more time to work out. You've got four inches on me but everyone in my family was a late developer. You favour your left knee very slightly which is the same knee I injured last year diving out of Doctor Nadir's blimp and…' she pointed down at Lucy's feet, 'you're wearing the boots I've wanted for the last year but aren't quite big enough to own yet. So come on, spill. What do you want?'

Lucy thought for a moment, folding her arms and tucking her hands into her sleeves, just as Ellie had done. Finally, she looked up at her younger self.

'You understand there are things I can't tell you.'

'I'll just guess them.'

'You'll guess wrong.'

'How do you know?'

'You honestly think I'll tell you?'

Ellie conceded the point and Lucy smiled. 'I'd forgotten how awkward I was. You're going to carry on his research and what you'll find… wow…' She looked out to sea and beyond it. 'We're entering a new age, Ellie. One filled with wonders that eclipse everything we've been taught. A new wave of exploration and understanding is sweeping out across the world and it starts here, and now, with you. You're going to hold every key and open every door and be magnificent and terrible and wonderful and it's all ahead of you.

Ellie folded her arms again. 'Bollocks.'

'I'm sorry?'

'No, you're bloody not! You knew I was going to say that and you knew I wouldn't buy the half-baked temporal bullshit you decided to peddle because you were too embarrassed to come here honestly. You came here, now, to see me, here, now, so once again, but slightly louder, what do you *want*?!'

Lucy opened her mouth, closed it again, and turned to the sea, her toe kicking at the ground. Ellie found herself doing the same thing and stopped before Lucy could see.

'I want you to do something else.'

'What?!'

Lucy swept an arm across the cemetery. '*Two hundred* extra bodies! Two *hundred*, Ellie! Almost everyone you meet will *die*. None of their deaths will be easy and none will be quick and some of them… some of them will be because of you. You're still young, you can still make a different choice.' There was something plaintive, desperate in her voice. 'I've seen things, Ellie, things that no one should have to see. I watched my best friend turn into glass, I saw St Paul's burn, and I was there when…' She blinked and set her jaw, a motion Ellie had seen a thousand times in the mirror.

'Don't be in Moscow next year. Just don't.'

Ellie blinked. 'You could warn them, you could stop it.'

'It's not my job.'

'And this is?'

'NO!' Her right arm swept upwards, taking in the span of the island behind them. 'Right now I'm supposed to be helping seal Moscow, visit the Comet Oracle, consult on an excavation in the Pacific Abyss and save my wife! None of which I would have to do if you *just turned away*!'

Ellie stood her ground, holding her older self's gaze. She watched the tears roll down Lucy's face, noticed with interest the star shaped scar on her temple, the slight discolouration around her eyes. She said nothing, and finally, Lucy spoke, her voice hollow and cracked.

'She's trapped. It's a pocket universe, on a wide temporal orbit. It only intersects with us once a year, but time moves faster there and she's been there a *year*. Please, Ellie, *please*. Do something else, *anything* else. I can't do—' Her voice broke again and she rubbed a hand fiercely over her eyes, turning away as she did so.

Ellie closed her eyes and rested her head against the thick, deep red leather of her jacket.

She blinked. 'That's a lot to think about.'

Lucy sagged with relief. 'I know it's a lot to take in.'

Ellie nodded. 'You're damn right it is, I mean, I didn't even know I was gay.'

Lucy blinked. 'Pardon me?'

'I suspected, of course. I thought I might be bisexual. Are we bisexual? Do we have boyfriends too?'

Lucy scowled. 'I should have known you wouldn't take this seriously.'

That was it. All the pent up rage, grief and frustration bubbled over and Ellie was moving, stalking towards her older self until she was an inch away, eyes blazing and fists bunched. 'I watched him *die*! For you that was God knows how many years ago but for me, it was last Tuesday so don't you *dare* say I'm not taking this seriously! You say our wife's trapped in a time loop? Then get her out! You do the job, whether it takes a day or a year but you do the *damn job*! Whatever! It! Takes! And from where I'm standing, that doesn't involve moping around on a sodden bloody graveyard on the worst day of your childhood with a bossy teenager who thinks she knows better than you!'

'Do you?' Lucy had barely spoken before Ellie slapped her. It was the blow meant for the priest and it knocked Lucy off her feet. She was up again in a second.

'You little bitch!'

Ellie smiled savagely, fists bunched, her guard up. Physical fights were *easy*. 'Decades younger *and* faster, so take your best shot.'

Lucy scowled and they stared at one another, Ellie silently begging her older self to try something. Finally, Lucy turned away. After a second, she began to cry. Ellie stared at her, and finally sat down too. She was surprised to hear her own voice crack when she spoke.

'The motto hasn't changed has it? The Institute's?'

'No.' Lucy's voice was hollow.

'Then what is it?'

'Per ardua ad conscentia.'

'Per ardua ad conscentia. I wanted to get a tattoo of that, you know.'

Lucy sniffed and then rolled her right sleeve up. The words gleamed silver on her forearm and Ellie tried very hard to focus on them and not the scars that ran under the fabric of her sleeve. Ellie forced a smile.

'What's her name?'

'Who?'

'Our wife?'

Lucy smiled. 'Her name is Moira.'

'Is she pretty?'

Lucy's smile widened. 'She's beautiful.'

Ellie clapped her hands together and stood. 'He told me, us, to always focus on beauty. You remember that?' Lucy sniffed and nodded. 'So you do that. You focus on Moira, and her smile, and her laugh and what she does for you and makes you feel. You do that, and you'll… we'll get her back. Now, how long have you got left? Until your tachyon charge runs out?'

Lucy stood, wiping her coat down. 'It doesn't work that way anymore. We can, um, we can stay as long as we like.'

Ellie looked around at the graves and the rolling country-side beneath them. On a hill at the far end of the island, the largest Van De Graaf generator on the planet crackled, its sparks brushing against the lowest of the clouds.

'The tea shop's pretty good.'

'Better in my day.'

'You're paying then. Grab us a table.'

Lucy was lying. It was exactly the polite lie Quantum would have used and, in realizing that, she knew why Lucy was lying. Ellie smiled, kissed her cheek and said 'Rescue Moira for us.'

Ellie Danger, Girl Daredevil, ran off, a streak of red leather and energy dancing through the gravestones. Lucy Tachyon, Queen of Time, watched her go, remembered how it had felt to hear everything she'd said, remembered forcing a smile when she'd seen the scars on her older self's arm and the immensely embarrassing conversation about her future sex life that she remembered looking forward to having.

She turned and looked at Niles Quantum's grave, as fresh as the memory of when he'd found her. The flattened ruins of Edinburgh had been abandoned by everyone but the last few, desperate rescue teams and Quantum had been amongst them. He'd found her huddled around the body of her father for warmth. He'd sat and talked with her, quietly explained what death meant and why it was not to be feared, told her the things she'd needed to hear, and finally carried her back to his tent. He was a giant angel, kind and funny and honest and brilliant and she'd told him, that first night, that she wished she could be just like him.

He'd looked at her for a long time and then told her to be careful what she wished for, because wishes had power, especially for little girls. Then he'd pulled a coin out of her right ear, a chocolate bar out of her left and let her sleep.

She thought about what she knew was coming, and what she knew had passed. She thought about the leather flight jacket and the plane that went with it, that in two days' time, Ellie would find out had been willed to her. She thought about Moira, beautiful, lost Moira, and for the first time, had an inkling of how she could be saved.

'Dangerous.' Professor Lucy Tachyon, Queen of Time, laughed as she said it, dusted herself off, took one last look around the past and smiled. There was a crackle of blue energy, the sound of a huge clock ticking, a tachyon SNAP! and she stepped back into tomorrow.

Father's Day

Francesca Terminiello

'Do you want to make a card for your daddy?'

The mid-morning sun gleamed off Mrs Fairbright's glasses and illuminated every strand of her yellow hair. She smelled of flowers and coffee.

'Okay,' said Molly, her fingers curled round a chubby black crayon.

Mrs Fairbright smiled and brought out a piece of royal blue card, carefully folded it down the middle and ran her thumb along the crease.

'Now, here's a stencil.' She produced a plastic template with a man-shaped hole and placed it over the card. 'Let's draw around the inside and you can start to make it look like Daddy.'

Tongue thrust between her lips, Molly carefully traced the shape.

'Well done, Molly, that looks fantastic,' said Mrs Fairbright. She rose from the tiny chair and her body creaked back up to full height. 'I'm just going to help Daniel. I'll be back soon.'

Molly stared at the outline, fingers already reaching for the pot of crayons. What colour should his hair be? Yellow, that was a nice, happy colour, like Mrs Fairbright's. Molly had brown curls like Mummy; perhaps Daddy should have bright yellow hair. She began hatching lines in all directions around the head. Wax built up in a thick halo, muddled with the black that was already there. Molly inspected the rest of the table: a pot of PVA glue that smelled like old fish, coloured tissue paper cut into small squares, a bowl of sequins the colours of jewels. Her nose almost touched the paper as she daubed some glue onto the face, and carefully chose from the selection. Two bright pink eyes shone back at her from the card and Molly smiled. It looked pretty.

She bent over the low table and continued to work.

'Oh that is fantastic,' gushed Mrs Fairbright, as she always did about everything. She placed a hand on Molly's back. 'Now, what does Daddy like? Does he like football? Racing cars?' The teacher showed Molly a paper plate of printed shapes: black and white footballs, cars, spades.

Molly stared.

'You choose what you think he'd like,' said Mrs Fairbright, before leaving once more to help Amelie who had spilt glue on her clothes.

Molly was completely absorbed by the task. She cut, glued, scribbled and sprinkled, until finally Mrs Fairbright picked the card up, beaming with pleasure.

'That is fan*tastic*, Molly, well done!' She shook off the excess glitter and held the card up as she turned so the rest of the children could see. Slack-jawed, they stared at the spangled colourful man who adorned the front of the card. 'Tell us about your daddy, Molly, what is he like?'

A jolt of energy shot through Molly's body. Mrs Fairbright's stare and the attention of all those faces, all at once, seemed to freeze her in place. Rather than blush she focused on the picture. What could she tell them about this man? Who was he? Molly had never known, Mummy never spoke of him, so she could just make it up. Right here, right now, she would decide who her daddy was, what he was like. It was a declaration, no longer her imagination.

If she said it now, in front of all these people, it would be real.

Molly took an audible breath. Mrs Fairbright, brows raised, nodded encouragement.

'My daddy,' said Molly, still looking at the picture 'is very clever.'

'Yes,' continued Mrs Fairbright 'and what does he do?' She

looked at the other children, then back to Molly, her smile always in place.

'He's . . .' Molly's mind spun through all the professions she could think of: doctor, fireman, policeman, astronaut '... a pirate.'

Mrs Fairbright's smile flickered for an instant.

'A pirate? Do you mean he's a pilot?'

Molly wasn't sure what a pilot was. She frowned.

Mrs Fairbright tried a different tactic.

'What does Daddy like to do?'

Molly wasn't exactly sure what a grown man would like to do, so she pondered her own favourite activities, then added a few she thought sounded about right.

'He likes running... and jumping and skipping and mountain climbing and football.'

'That's just lovely.' Mrs Fairbright beamed at her.

That night, as Molly lay in bed, she cuddled Tansy, her favourite doll, and twisted the woollen hair between her fingers. In her mind she went through everything about her daddy that had been left out, everything Mrs Fairbright hadn't asked her.

He was good at dancing.

He was clean.

He smelled of flowers.

He would sing when Mummy was sad.

She thought about Mummy a moment. What would Mummy like him to be? Mummy hated washing up, so he'd have to be good at that. She liked to watch Eastenders so he'd have to know everything about that too.

He had to be kind.

And buy lots of chocolate

And wine. Mummy liked wine.

And he would never say bad words.

Molly continued to add to her list, her fingers working and twisting Tansy's hair, until her eyes closed.

Alex switched off the TV, just as the tom-tom beats pounded out and the aerial view of the twisting Thames slid across the screen. She yawned and stood, shuffling into the kitchen in slippered feet, mug and plate in one hand. The lives of the characters were always so tumultuous. They never seemed to show the boring bits, but then Alex supposed that just wouldn't make good television. Better the drama happened to them than her. She just wanted her bed.

In the corner of the kitchen she spotted Molly's bag, unzipped and stuffed full of that day's drawings from pre-school. Alex sighed as she started to rifle through the bag and stack up her daughter's prodigious efforts.

Earlier that afternoon Julie had picked Molly up as usual and when Alex had finished her shift and gone to collect her she had kissed and hugged the little girl, fresh in her pyjamas, ready for the drive home. Sometimes Molly would talk about what she had done that day, but today she had fallen asleep almost before the car had left Julie's road.

Alex went through the pile of pictures: a car, a sort of Rorschach collection of splodges, a fairy and some flowers. Another took some turning before she worked out it was a dinosaur.

Then she felt the edges of a card. *Oops, I'm not meant to see this yet.*

Alex grinned. She couldn't help but think of Molly's earnest little face when she handed her the card. A cloud of glitter tumbled through the air, some small pieces trickled to the bottom of the rucksack and dusted the floor. The card was thick with glue and decoration. Alex was scared to knock some of it off and handled it gingerly. She wondered what occasion this was for. Mother's Day had already been, so had Easter, her birthday was in January and Christmas was months away.

She turned it over.

HAPPY FATHERS DAY read printed words pasted across the page.

Alex froze. Her mind momentarily raced through wild possibilities, lurching from one to the next. They all pointed to the same thing: Craig had contacted their daughter, he was in Molly's life.

She felt her heart thud as she studied the picture. Her skin was hot. The image was a sparkling gingerbread man, that was the only way she could describe it. Molly had put in a lot of time and effort with this one, it was obvious from the amount of detail and variety. The other pictures were disposable, things she churned out and forgot instantly, but this was something very important to her.

Guilt clawed at Alex. Maybe she should have explained more. She'd decided to wait until Molly was older, unable to explain to a four year old that her daddy didn't want anything to do with her or her mummy. She couldn't think of a way to say it that didn't make her sound wronged. Craig wasn't a bad person, just useless at relationships. They had only been together for a couple of months when Alex became pregnant. After she told him he'd become more and more withdrawn, until eventually she realised he wasn't going to stay.

She'd been angry, and hurt, but in the end she knew it was for the best. She couldn't bring herself to get rid of the baby, though. She didn't know when she would get another chance to have a child.

By the time Molly was born Craig had moved towns, Alex lost all contact with him and was actually relieved he wanted no part in Molly's life. This made her feel guilty more than anything, but a large part of her was proud, proud to take all of the responsibility for Molly's care and upbringing, to show the world that she could do this on her own.

Since Craig there had been one or two dates, but none had been serious. Alex knew it wasn't because she was a single mother or anything like that, she just hadn't felt anything for them. She would grow old single, it wouldn't matter. She would be free, and she would get all the love she needed from Molly.

She opened the card

'Love Molly xxxxxxxxxxxxxxxxxxxxxxxxxxxxxxxxxx' covered the interior. Alex sighed and sagged as she considered: if Craig had spoken to Molly she wouldn't have been able to keep it to herself. All the children must have done these, why would Molly sit out and refuse? It was an activity like any

other. She smiled, stacked the pictures neatly and put them in a drawer, before carefully returning the Father's Day card to the bag. She would hate Molly to think she had found something secret.

'Mummy?' said Molly, poking at her Cheerios.

'Yes darling?' Alex called as she stood before the living room mirror and busily scraped up her hair.

'When is Father's Day?'

'Erm, I'm not sure.'

She grabbed her phone off the mantelpiece, hair held up with the other hand, and thumbed the search into Google. After she had told Molly the date the little girl replied:

'Is that today?'

'No, it's tomorrow. Come on, eat up quick, we'll be late for Julie.'

Mrs Fairbright gathered the children together, coated and booted with bags by their sides as they sat, legs crossed and fidgeting, in the story corner.

'Make sure you remember to give your daddies their cards everybody... Oh, look, here come your mummies and daddies now!'

The door opened and parents entered the room, arms outstretched. One by one the children were summoned by Mrs Fairbright to dive into the waiting embraces. Molly watched as some of the fathers were given their cards, and she only smiled at their smiles. *My daddy will be really pleased with his card too.*

Soon enough, though, Julie appeared. She smiled, and beckoned with an outstretched hand, several shopping bags and her keys dangled from the other.

'Come on then, poppet.'

In the car Molly sulked. She really had thought her daddy would collect her that afternoon. She pulled Tansy out of her bag and started to twiddle her hair.

'Everything alright, Molly?'

Julie's eyes, wrinkled at the corners, studied Molly through the rear-view mirror.

'Yes.'

Julie was quiet for a few seconds. Molly thought for a moment that she understood.

'Good, we've got fish fingers for tea when we get in.' She cranked the handbrake as she pulled over. 'I just need to stop at the post office first. You wait here, I won't be long.'

Julie's perfume lingered in the car. Molly twirled and twirled Tansy's hair, staring out the window as rain began to patter on the glass. It made her feel very sleepy. Then a figure appeared, approaching Julie's car with a bright, warm smile. He waved. Molly waved back. He started jumping, as high as he could, colours streaming all around him as he flew. Molly noticed that despite the rain he looked surprisingly well dressed, his brightly coloured clothes spotless, and his hair, although very yellow, with smudges of black here and there, stuck out in all directions. It made her giggle. When he saw her laughing the man pulled a funny face, and his pink eyes glittered. They looked pretty. He opened the driver's door, got in the seat and turned back to Molly, pulling on the seatbelt with a click.

'Ahoy there, little lady. What say we set sail for adventure?'

Molly giggled again, but said nothing. She held Tansy's head over her mouth. The man reached out for the doll and Molly let him take her. She laughed with delight as he made the toy talk.

'I say it's an excellent plan, Daddy!' squeaked Tansy.

'Well shiver me timbers!' said Daddy. He stared at Tansy, holding her at arm's length. 'You can join my crew, Tansy.'

'How do you know her name?' asked Molly, finding her voice through the laughter.

'I'm your daddy, I know everything about you.'

He grinned, handed her back the doll, and started the engine.

The CompaniSIM, The Treasure, The Thief and Her Sister

C.J. Paget

Isabella Sauber understands the mansion's security setup at a glance. She knows how the security firms think, she's read their manuals of best practices, she knows just where to look to find the cameras and sensors. But her professional interest, and the alarm systems, are wasted here: There's nothing left to steal. The interior of the great old house has been stripped bare, everything sold or repossessed. All that's left are stacks of technology no-one wants any more: plastic modules of all shapes and sizes and styles, wired together in huddles of blinking, coloured lights.

Marcus-Sebastian leads her swiftly through the sanctuary's echoing rooms, through huge French windows, and out into the building's grounds. The gardens have fared better than the house itself, and are lush and blooming with all the colours of spring. An army of little crab-shaped robots clip hedges and weed flowerbeds. But some of these are clearly malfunctioning: they chase each other in circles or are, apparently, dancing.

Marcus-Sebastian turns his grey-dreadlocked head to

examine her with tired, untrusting eyes. 'They're here,' he says. 'You have only to connect to the local network.'

Isabella thinks a command which activates implants in her brain and opens her cerebellum to the virtual world. A cheerful logon-chime bings in her mind's ear and they are no longer alone. Now she sees wine gum-coloured dragons and pink elephants and glowing-eyed robots that chase each other in circles, or dance to unheard music, or hover over the crab-like task-drones, guiding them through the work of clipping hedges or weeding flowerbeds. All of them are a little transparent, a polite convention so one can tell the virtual from the physical. Isabella is faintly alarmed to discover they have a coterie of fairies and *kawaii* aliens walking along with them. These are the pushy ones, the smart ones; they understand why she's here. They jostle back and forth, images overlapping, all big cartoon eyes and smiles, doing their virtual best to look adorable.

'Guys, could we have some privacy?' says Marcus-Sebastian.

The mob breaks up, its members waving cheery goodbyes as they disperse through the garden. Isabella fights down a shudder: She's always found virtual characters creepy but can't let Marcus-Sebastian see that. 'I see some are eager to find a new home?' she says.

'Companisims are made to provide companionship,' says Marcus-Sebastian. 'The need is coded deep within them. But I think some of them see how things are going. I'm supporting so many they only get one timeshared day online a month, and I can't afford the processing time to do any better. I'm broke and it costs a lot to keep this many companisims running at any one time. I won't be able to do it much longer.'

'Would that be so bad?' asks Isabella. 'I mean they'll still be there, just... asleep?'

'How would you feel about sleep, if you might never wake up again?'

Isabella resists answering. She wants to tell the man he's an idiot, to remind him that these are just advanced toys, cartoon characters no more real than the children's fantasies they resemble. But he's clearly too far gone in his delusions and shaking him out of them isn't part of Isabella's plan.

Marcus-Sebastian pauses before a two-foot-high cartoon robot complete with key turning in its back. It floats above a task-drone, which copies its movements so that together they can perform the task of pruning a shrub. The companisim's ridiculous cartoon face is set in an expression of furious concentration, but the shrub has still been mangled.

'That's very good, Gizmo,' says Marcus-Sebastian. 'You can go play with the others now.'

The task-drone slumps into inactivity. The transparent cartoon robot throws up its arms and announces 'Gizmo!' before racing off as fast as his little mechanical legs will carry him.

'He's getting better,' says Marcus-Sebastian, ruefully examining the assaulted shrub. 'He's not cutting them off at the roots anymore. I'll get one of the others to tidy it up.'

'You make them do chores?' asks Isabella.

'Yes,' says Marcus-Sebastian. 'It's important they have responsibilities. They're always learning, you know. For some of them the change is hard to spot, but they're all growing, all learning, all the time. Some of them just learn slowly.'

'That one spoke, but the others are all silent?' says Isabella.

'That's his one word,' says Marcus-Sebastian. 'They're almost all mute and most of them have deep-wired grammar blockers, so they can read but not form English sentences. We didn't want them passing any Turing tests, you see. 'Course, the truth came out in the end, but now they're recognized as sentients no-one wants them, and there's nowhere for them to go.'

'You used to make them?'

'Yes.'

'Not proud of it?'

'No,' says Marcus-Sebastian. 'It's funny how a nine-figure salary helps one rationalize things. I told myself I was making toys, but instead I was making slaves.'

Isabella is curious how deep the fellow's madness goes.

'Slaves? That's rather strong. Surely it's no worse than keeping pets?'

'If we could take their grammar blockers out and they started speaking, you wouldn't feel that way,' says Marcus-Sebastian.

'Which ones are the fastest learners?' asks Isabella.

Marcus-Sebastian narrows his eyes a little. 'Why is that important? What are you hoping to get out of this?'

'I'm a woman of a certain age in search of a companion.'

'Join a bridge club.'

'I tried that. Truth is, I don't like people. They make you a pawn in their private chess game. They're unfaithful. They let you down.'

Marcus-Sebastian stares into her face like he's reading something etched on the bones of her skull. Isabella smiles back: A thief must be a mistress of the innocent smile. She knows he's desperate to find homes for at least some of his charges. Eventually he says, 'Come and meet Wend-E, she's about the smartest. Advanced model intended for the, um, the mature female demogra-'

'The spinster market,' says Isabella, sensing the chance to put him a little off-balance.

'Uh, yes.' He leads her across the garden. 'She can play all board and card games to a high standard and is an expert in a number of arts and crafts, making her a capable tutor in everything except languages.'

'Can she learn new skills too?'

'If you provide her with enough input and data space, yes. I'll be sad to see her go, she's a big help with keeping the others in line. Some of them have deep-coded mischief engrams to make them more entertaining. Not so entertaining when you've got a houseful of them.' He stops walking, gives Isabella that searching look again. 'Wend-E had some... bad experiences with her previous people,' he says. 'It's taken a long time for me to get her to trust humans again.'

Isabella smiles and nods, but says nothing.

Marcus calls one of the companisims over to join them. It looks something like a five-year-old girl's first drawing of herself, if the five year-old were good with 3D-graphics. She has a head like a white egg lying on its side, between bunches of something that's clearly supposed to be pink hair. The eyes, mouth and eyebrows are stencilled in big black pixels, as though on an ancient LCD display. Whoever designed her thought that blinking and constantly raised eyebrows were cute. She doesn't walk to them, she skips. She's quite the most repellent thing Isabella has ever seen.

'Wend-E, this is Isabella,' says Marcus-Sebastian.

The companisim performs a virtual curtsey, smiles, and blinks her cartoon eyes, each blink accompanied by a soft 'plink' sound.

'Wend-E, you've been with us a long time,' says Marcus-Sebastian, 'and I know you're happy here-'

Wend-E nods her oval head vigorously.

'But this lady is looking for a companion. Are you interested?'

Wend-E turns her big LCD eyes to Isabella. They go 'plink, plink'. The black mouth line turns up, a little uncertainly, into a pixelated smile.

Isabella Sauber smiles back till her cheek muscles ache.

The companisim module is big, the size of a wine-crate. It has an array of plug-in ports on one face and a little motion-effect picture of a waving Wend-E on all the others. When Marcus-Sebastian handed it to her, he gave Isabella a final, long look, and for a second she thought he'd snatch it back, but she smiled and smiled, and eventually he let it go. It's the closest thing Wend-E has to a physical body, and it's now one part of a cluster of devices filling the main room of Isabella's apartment. It sits within the frame of a portable neuro-surgery array, and cables snake from it to a Lamsam Industries simularium, one of the top-drawer models they use for big virtual events.

Isabella makes some final adjustments then sits on her sofa with her eyes closed, activates her neural implants, and drifts out of this reality and into the virtual reality of the simularium. In that empty world she is an omnipresent goddess, and the only other thing in there is the shape of a cartoon girl floating like a doll discarded in deep space. Isabella thinks a command, and waits while symbology scrolls across Wend-E's eggshell face; boot messages and software patent warnings in a grab-bag of languages. The black eyes and mouth appear, just sketched flat lines, then the eyes 'open' and blink. *Plink, plink.*

'You're wired into a petabyte simularium,' says Isabella, her voice filling this little world like thunder.

Wend-E 'looks' about at her blank universe. A question-mark appears where her nose would be.

'This will be your training-ground. I'm afraid it's not a companion I need, it's an accomplice. I am a thief, one of the better ones currently alive. When I began it was still a time when a lone gunwoman could get by, but as security got more complex and my ambitions grew I had to start assembling teams. Alas, as the locks have gotten better and better, the standard of the modern criminal has steadily declined. You can't get the help nowadays, people always let you down. I need someone I can control, someone who can compromise military-grade countermeasures. No human is competent to do this anymore, but an A.I., even a low-grade commercial companion model, moves and lives in the world of data. You're going to help me pull off the most important heist of my life, in which I hope to reclaim something very dear to me. You'll handle the virtual world while I deal with the physical. I know you don't currently have those skill sets, but you're a fast learner and I've created a suitable teaching environment.'

Wend-E's question-mark nose becomes an exclamation point.

'To provide you with suitable motivation, I have mounted your physical component within one of those x-ray arrays normally used in neuro-surgery. Every time you fail to perform to my expectations, I will use it to destroy one junction in your neural net. If you consistently perform poorly you'll gradually lose all your memories and inbuilt skill sets, until you completely cease to function at all.'

The companisim's cartoon eyes get bigger, and the mouth line turns into an arc like a very miserable monochrome rainbow.

'We will begin immediately,' says Isabella. Structures rise around Wend-E, filling the other-space of the simularium, forming a maze around the companisim's avatar. 'This maze contains locks and tripwires which you must overcome in order to escape THESE.'

Two flaming hellhounds ripped from an immersim game blaze into snarling existence. Wend-E backs away from them, LCD eyes wide. They spring. Wend-E runs, flapping her cartoon arms like she's trying to take flight. The first trap pops up before her: an access gateway keyed to refuse Wend-E's UID. It takes Wend-E an instant to morph into a pink demon, presenting a false identity, and she's through the gate and off down the paths of the labyrinth, pursued by the hounds.

'Good,' murmurs Isabella Sauber, 'very good.' She opens a bag of rice crackers and settles down to watch Wend-E running like a very scared rat through a virtual maze.

For the first two weeks, Wend-E's learning performance exceeds Isabella's expectations. But as the tasks get more difficult, Wend-E's progress slows. Isabella begins to grow frustrated: It's not like they have all the time in the world. Every day new security measures are created, every day the task she's training Wend-E for gets tougher. And it's not just the companisim who is growing steadily more obsolete.

Isabella nurtures her anger, stoking it like a fire. At first, like any fire, it's hard to get going; she's too ready to excuse the companisim's failings. But she tells herself one must be tough. She institutes a regime of punishments, starting slight, using each as a stepping-stone to a greater cruelty. She obsesses over Wend-E's failures, ignores its successes, mutters to herself that the virtual being is wilful, lazy, conspiring against her. The fire in her soul begins to catch, flicker and flare.

Ignition finally comes one day when Wend-E repeatedly fails to complete a particular maze within time. Isabella, watching through her neural implants from the comfort of her sofa, allows the companisim thirteen tries before she slaps a hand down on the arm of the sofa and shouts, 'Too slow!'. The impact bounces the glass of green tea that was resting within easy reach straight into her lap, raising a furious screech. 'Now look what you've made me do, you stupid-'

In her virtual dungeon Wend-E collapses to her virtual knees and covers her shaking eggshell head with cartoon hands. She's still like that when Isabella comes back from changing into a different set of jeans.

'Stop that,' hisses Isabella, legs still stinging from the scalding tea, and fury blazing bright within her. 'You're nothing but a lot of connections in a nanotronic core, you're all fake, so stop trying to garner my sympathy. Stand up.'

Wend-E stands on shaking legs but keeps her head down as though to hide the black LCD tears running down her face in repeated patterns.

'Now, I explained this,' says Isabella. 'If you don't perform you'll be punished. It's you that's making this happen by your repeated failures, it's not my fault. As previous punishments have been too random for you to care, I've analysed some of the linkages in your neural net, and mapped your memories within it.' Suddenly Wend-E is not alone. In the simulation with her are the frozen images of pink elephants, paper tigers, clockwork robots and cutesy aliens. Even Gizmo is there.

'From now on, every time you fail I will destroy the memory of one of your little friends. You get to choose which one.'

Wend-E shakes her head, refusing to even look at the choices laid out before her.

'Choose, or I'll wipe all of them.'

It's two months before Wend-E runs all the training mazes in an acceptable time. A week after that Isabella puts Wend-E through a vast and malignant training sim that auto-learns Wend-E's responses, so the companisim can never use the same trick twice. These days Isabella has to watch Wend-E's performance at one hundredth speed, otherwise her meat-slow perceptions would see only a blur. Wend-E changes appearance as she dons false identities, swarms as she forks copies of herself to work in parallel or act as decoys, casts lightning when she conjures intrusion programs, and performs complex dances in shifting helixes of light whose purpose Isabella cannot imagine. She completes Isabella's bastard-level simulation significantly under the expected time. Wend-E has become a maestro of deception and sabotage, able to invent solutions in milliseconds. She's ready, and it's only cost the memories of six of her friends from the sanctuary, along with some skill-sets that Isabella deemed unimportant, including two of Wend-E's favourite dances.

Wend-E stands like a soldier on a parade ground, but with her eggshell head turned down, staring at her cartoon shoes, awaiting the judgement on her performance.

'Excellent. You're finally ready,' Isabella tells her. 'The time has come to discuss our true objective.'

A blue sea unfurls around Wend-E, filling the simularium like an azure carpet rolling out. In this sea, trailing a shining wake like a bridal train, is a huge, wedge-shaped, flat-topped ship. An aircraft carrier, though most of the flight-deck has been repurposed into a landscaped garden with swimming pools and tennis courts. The only concession to aircraft is a helipad at one end.

'The Villa Wanderlust: Formerly the HMS Queen Elizabeth, 'till the British had to sell their military to bail out their banking system, and now the world's most vulgar celebrity crib. Home to the world's most successful corporate parasite: Nicola Sauber. My sister.' The carrier splits into full-motion cutaway, displaying a labyrinth of internal compartments. 'It's been retrofitted with a modern pebble-bed reactor and mostly stays in international waters and out of reach of any law. Inside there's ballrooms, cinemas, gyms, and a private museum stocked with art treasures, including this.'

The Villa Wanderlust vanishes, replaced by a large, ornate, wooden desk-globe.

'My mother was a very successful antiquities dealer. The house was full of old things. And there was one thing that I loved: This. I used to trace the outlines of continents with my fingers, reading the names of mythical places, speaking them out loud. The whole world in my hands, and I travelled it all in my dreams. It should have come to me when Mother died. But that bitch came along and wormed her way into Mother's heart, and set her against me. After that I never did anything right, and Mother cut me off. I've stolen diamonds, national secrets and holy relics, but I never wanted those things for myself. Tonight I'm taking this back. It's the last thing left of my mother. So don't fuck up, okay?'

Wend-E nods, but her LCD expression is anything but okay.

The sky above the container-port is the colour of a television switched off, scrapped and buried in landfill: It's night. Isabella scans the port from the concealment of a concrete storage hut, flattened against it so the bioware pigmentation layer of her custom-made stealth-suit can blend her into her surroundings like an octopus. A headband of tiny cameras relay image-enhanced infra-red through her neural implants, giving her better sight than owls or cats. She sees a couple of ageing bulk-carrier vessels slumbering in the dock, but no living thing moves except the occasional rat. Tonight it's the final of the Pan Africa League Championships, and the port's watchmen have hacked the SCADA monitoring screens to accept a pay-per-view web feed, just as Isabella had hoped.

One forty-foot, steel shipping container rests at the centre of an 'X' of reflective mirror-crete, awaiting pickup.

Isabella looks down to where Wend-E is pressed against the hut, a crudely rendered black scarf wrapped about her head, ninja style. 'Are you mocking me?' thinks Isabella.

The oval head shakes swiftly from side to side.

'Then what are you doing? You've no need to hide. Only I can see you, you're just an image in my neural implants.' If Wend-E can be said to be physically anywhere right now, then she's locked in the boot of Isabella's nearby car. Her hardware module is one component in an array of humming technologies, including a long-range net-node that communicates on an encrypted channel with Isabella's neural implants. 'Take that silly scarf off. This isn't a game. If you fuck up, there's no going back, and if I don't come back safe and sound you'll be stuck here forever, or at least until they find my car and tow it away to be crushed. Do you understand?'

Wend-E sullenly nods her eggshell head, then looks sharply up and out to sea, cartoon eyes widening. Though she sees and hears through Isabella's implant-mediated senses, Wend-E hears it first. Moments later so does Isabella. A distant throb, as though a giant fast-beating heart were drifting over the sea towards them.

'Right on time,' thinks Isabella. She breaks cover and sprints to the shipping container. The electronic entry-code lock is a standard type with a well-known vulnerability. Isabella has broken so many of these locks that the procedure requires no actual thought. She cuts an access-hole in the steel, bridges the current-carrying cables so the electronics think they're still delivering power to the locking mechanism, and isolates the magnetic latch. 'Chunk' says the door, and it slides open easily. Isabella slips in, shutting it swiftly behind her. Wend-E steps through the closed steel door like a very short ghost. Isabella unclips a glove from her stealth-suit. Her hand is like a flaming torch in her infra-red vision. It's enough illumination to see the contents of the shipping container.

It's empty.

'What the hell?' murmurs Isabella.

Wend-E looks curiously up at her, plinking her LCD eyes.

'This should be full of stuff for my sister. Provisions, luxuries, expensive clothes she'll never bother to wear. Something's-'

Clang! The container reverberates as something strikes its

walls, and then Isabella's guts go weightless: They're being lifted into the sky.

'We proceed as planned,' thinks Isabella. She reopens the container door, and is greeted with gale-force winds and a sound like a thunderstorm trying to fight its way out of an echo-chamber. Their container has been seized by a freight gyrocopter, an automated model as smart as a homing pigeon, and they are being carried back to its roost.

Isabella clambers swiftly up onto the roof of the shipping container, enjoying the battle against the monster wind. Without her suit's grip-surfaces she'd be blown through the night and down to the sunless sea. As it is, the high-speed crawl along the container's steel roof is as strenuous as any cliff-face climb. Isabella feels a fierce satisfaction. *I'm not too old for this yet.* Few people could do this within the required time limit. Every second is taking them further from the long-range comms unit in her car. In order for Wend-E to stay with her, they need a more powerful transceiver than Isabella's implants. The copter's communications are their only hope. She climbs one of the insectile legs that grips the shipping container, pushing the envelope of recklessness, barely able to hold on in the rotor-wash. Wend-E floats in the air beside her, unable to do anything until Isabella establishes communications with the copter's puny nanotronic brain. At the top of her climb Isabella finds the Standard Diagnostic Port in the copter's spindly body. She pulls a disk-shaped limpet net-node from her belt and slaps it on the wall, where it sticks while she pulls a cable-jack from it and plugs it into the port.

Wend-E dives into the net-node, passing ghostlike through it and into the airframe of the copter itself. Isabella's virtual vision depicts Wend-E inside the craft's body, negotiating virtual gateways, casting code as she fights miniature battles within the craft's tiny brain, changing shape as she presents false identities to the copter's security. Isabella holds her breath, aware they must be close to the range limit of the communications unit in her car. Wend-E must gain control of the copter's communications to maintain contact. The companisim tells the copter she's a systems security audit and three diagnostic routines, which manifests to Isabella as Wend-E's doll-like avatar trying on various carnival masks. A fractal gateway opens, and Wend-E steps through, and reappears sat in an imaginary pilot's chair within the nose of the aircraft. She has control and establishes a high-quality link to her physical component in the boot of Isabella's car. The copter is now their communications hub and mission control.

'Don't break anything in there, or this'll become a submarine,' mutters Isabella.

Out in the vast darkness, a light twinkles on the surface of the sea. Isabella scrambles back down the copter's leg, heading back to the concealment of the shipping container. In her mind's eye she sees Wend-E working the copter's communications, arms blurring as she manipulates flowing, glowing streams of code, downloading instruments of intrusion into the aircraft's data space, from where she'll use them to attack the Villa Wanderlust itself.

The storm of rotors changes pitch as the copter throttles back for landing. Isabella holds the container door a little open so she can watch their descent towards the festival of light that is the Wanderlust after dark. The ship's deck is buried beneath a verdant paradise of palm trees, streams vaulted by pretty little bridges, fountains, pools and pagodas. Only the white control towers betray that somewhere under all this is the cold steel of a flight deck. Isabella realises that in all her adult life she's never owned so much as a shrub, while her sister owns a floating Eden.

The aircraft alights so perfectly that Isabella never feels the touchdown. The gyrocopter creaks and servos whine as its rotors and engine-pods fold out of harm's way for the ride on one of the two aircraft lifts to the hanger deck. Wend-E is still battling as the carrier swallows them. She must at least gain control of the security in the hanger deck before Isabella can leave the container.

The door to Isabella's shipping-crate prison unlatches. She flattens herself against a steel wall, her stealth-suit matching its colour and texture. An autonomous forklift rolls into the container, carrying a small piano. Isabella wonders that Nicola would discard such a thing: maybe she's bought a better one. Overlaid upon the real world Isabella sees four Wend-Es dancing around the forklift, each trying different techniques to subvert it, but getting no response. The lumbering machine is too dumb to be hacked. If Wend-E is trying this she must have failed to break into the ship's systems via communications and is trying other avenues.

Wend-E has the copter register a complaint about one of the tip-jets misfiring. Answering that call comes a service drone that looks like a Jack-in-the-box on wheels, if Jack were a metal velociraptor. The gyrocopter unfolds its rotors for inspection, and the service drone cranes up to study the jets at their tips. An image of Wend-E appears standing on one rotor. She bends down and starts feeding the drone something with a spoon. Whatever intrusion method this represents, it seems to work, because when the service drone rolls away once more, Wend-E is riding on it.

There's the distinctive 'snap' of a large circuit breaker tripping, and the deck lighting goes out. Wend-E's image appears, beckoning Isabella from her hiding place. Isabella crouch-runs towards a hatchway, beyond which is light and...

Carpets. She steps into a corridor that once heard the call to battle stations, but is now burdened with deep-pile carpet and tasteful lighting. *Not so much swords-into-ploughshares, as swords-into-evening-gowns,* thinks Isabella, *and vulgar as hell.* Wend-E must have control of local security, for she beckons Isabella along the decorated corridors. But Isabella goes cautiously: Even though she's seen so much automation, there must be people here. Nicola was never a hermit. She passes ballrooms and boardrooms and banqueting halls. She imagines the life her sister lives here: Important meetings to which she was never invited, glittering parties to which she was never invited, debased orgies to which she was never invited. Envy boils in the witch's cauldron of her heart. She notices dust on the furnishings. Nicola has probably forgotten she even owns some of these rooms.

Eventually Isabella arrives at the holy of holies, doors of tastefully tinted bullet-resistant glass, the entry to Nicola's private museum. In the world of data and security systems Isabella sees Wend-E has multiplied herself throughout the portion of the ship's systems she now controls. A thousand floating Wend-Es assault the museum doors. The companisim is evidently trying to brute-force her way past this particular barrier, to overwhelm the security with a million requests for entry. Isabella can only crouch and wait; and hope that nothing goes wrong.

The museum's doors swing open and Wend-E collects her many selves back into one image and floats through. Isabella follows into a space almost totally dark but for uplighters illuminating relics and artefacts within glass cases: treasures seen only by Nicola and her sycophants. Centre stage is taken by some hideous chunk of cubist overindulgence, an affront that makes Isabella gasp out loud, thinking: *Why is **this** in pride of place? Where is our mother's legacy?*

Isabella has to search for her target, and for panicked moments she thinks it's not here. But in the end she finds it, shunted into a corner, labelled simply 'Globe. Circa 1800.' Isabella looks down on the sepia shapes of Russia, Mongolia, China and India. Childhood memories surge up from their burial places and she recalls running her finger along the crenelated edges of continents, imagining her fingertip was an airliner bound for places with hard-to-read names. She realizes the horrible truth; that it was the last time she was happy, and here is the last fragment of that time, kept imprisoned and forgotten in a dark corner under a three-word description. Nicola clearly cares nothing for it and only keeps it to deprive her sister.

Looking about, Isabella sees Wend-E's LCD face peering back at her from every corner of the room, floating superimposed over every hidden camera and passive infra-red sensor, big black eyes going 'plink, plink'. 'Is it safe?' Isabella asks.

The many Wend-Es nod vigorously. She's in control of the room's security systems.

Isabella steps to the globe's glass prison. Her heart beats, her skin heats. She reaches out trembling hands, feeling the edges of the case, seeking its weaknesses and entry points.

She sees the camera-lens looking out at her like the black eye of a rattlesnake, and knows instantly what it means. The case has its own in-built security, disconnected from all networks like a tiny private universe, or Wend-E would already have dealt with it. But to what purpose? By now Wend-E is in control of so much of the ship that it's too late to issue a warning signal. Surely nothing can stop them now?

The floor of the case splits and folds, moving with clockwork smoothness. Isabella draws a sharp breath, and it's as loud as a shout in the silence of the room. Arms bearing fanged wheels rise out of the depths of the case. Isabella only has time to scream 'No!' as the wheels spin up, before they touch wood and sawdust plumes within the case like blood in water. She smashes her fist against the toughened glass, claws at it, screeching, as the antique globe explodes into a whirling maelstrom of splinters and broken pieces. Then the rending clawed arms retreat, leaving Isabella looking down at a mound of kindling and tan dust.

'Hello, sister,' says a voice in her head.

Isabella feels a coldness prickle across her back, for though she heard the voice through her neural implants, it still maps to a position in the real world… right behind her.

She turns.

Nicola Sauber stands, arms crossed and head tilted, smiling knowingly. She's slightly transparent and her feet don't touch the ground. She's a projection, something conveyed into Isabella's implants through the ship's data-systems. So Wend-E is not in complete control after all. 'Knew you'd come for it one day,' says Nicola.

'Why?' asks Isabella. 'Why? It was our mother's.' She realises there are tears on her face, wipes them away furiously.

'Because it's the last remnant of our childhood, of a world you tried to force me out of. You hated me from the moment I was born. I was competition, and you've never been able to stand that, always thought you were entitled to everything by birth. I had to work to get noticed, I had to work for everything. You expected everything to be given to you. That's why I built an empire, and you're a common thief. That's why Mother liked me more. All I ever wanted was a sister like other girls had, but I had you. You made me hate you, I didn't want to do it. You taught me, trained me, made me in your image. And I carried that darkness inside me all my life, unable to really trust anyone.'

'Oh, always the victim!' says Isabella, throwing up her hands. 'The one role you play really well! You're richer than fruitcake but still deprived!'

'Riches aren't much use to the dead.'

'Dead?' says Isabella, 'No, this is one of your tricks.'

'No tricks. Five years now. Cancer. That's what a lifetime of hating does to you. My money keeps the machines running, keeps the empire online, like the Soviet Union after Stalin died.'

'Then who am I speaking to?'

'No-one. Just a ghost, a simulation. Guaranteed non-sentient or it'd be illegal, though I don't understand how they can guarantee that. Supposedly it predicts with high accuracy what I would do and say in this situation. The game's over, sister, and at least I died rich. What have you got?'

'Oh, you always had to have the last word-'

'I'll have better than that, sister dear. Because there's one great advantage to being dead.' The smile widens, revealing perfect, virtual, teeth. 'You can't be tried for murder.'

The floor beneath Nicola's feet folds away just like the interior of the globe's display case. Isabella watches, startled, as all the display cases sink into recesses in the deck, like they know trouble's coming and are slinking away to hide. Through the opening beneath Nicola's floating image a familiar figure rises: Black Edo-period Tosei-gusoku armour, topped with a horned helmet. Isabella steps away from it, eyes widening.

'Oh yes, this fell on you when you were seven, didn't it?' sneers Nicola's ghost. 'You were terrified of it ever after. Mother had to get rid of it to stop the nightmares. Took a lot to find it. I've made some alterations, of course.'

Red LEDs illuminate in the helmet, forming ridiculous

horror-movie eyes like something from a cheap theme-park. It should be laughable but the smell of lacquered iron unlocks forgotten terrors that rise up out of Isabella's guts and strangle her reason. A tide of irrational childhood fear breaks over her, and she's drowning.

The armour moves, whipping an antique blade up and into a guard position with a faint whirr of servos. A shriek echoes through the room, and Isabella sees her screaming face reflected in the sword's mirror-smooth surface. The sound is coming from her. She throws herself sideways as the sword scythes down, singing through the still air. She lands hard on the tile floor and scrambles up and away. The animate armour raises its blade and marches after her with the comic clockwork gait of a child's toy. Isabella looks about for an escape, a weapon, anything, but the room is empty and the door sealed and Wend-E has vanished from her mind's eye. She can run from this thing, but she knows it will march after her in endless, ever-decreasing circles until she falls down, exhausted. It's futile.

She does it anyway. Her sister's ghost watches with a Mona Lisa smile as the clockwork assassin chases Isabella about the room. It doesn't take long for fearful flesh to fade and falter, to become clumsy and slow. The sword slashes, Isabella dodges, the sword twists and stabs, and its point enters her thigh. Her leg collapses under her and Isabella finds herself sitting in a spreading pool of blood. The armour raises its sword to slice her in two...

...and stops. Freezes in that position. The LED eyes flicker like activity lights on a net-node. In her implant-enhanced mind's eye Isabella sees Wend-E standing over her, arms outstretched like a wizard commanding a demon.

'What's this?' says Nicola's ghost. She crouches to bring her face level with Wend-E's determined LCD visage. 'And who are you, little one?'

There seems to be a reply, though Isabella doesn't hear it.

'She hurt you, didn't she?' says Nicola's ghost, translucent face a portrait of maternal concern. Isabella remembers this.

Even when she was flesh, Nicola could turn emotions on and off like stage-show lighting.

Wend-E's eggshell head nods miserably. Nicola leans like an actor pretending to listen to a rag-doll in an old children's program. 'She did all that? How wicked. But now the boot is on the other foot. How would you like to choose which bits we cut out first, while she screams and screams?'

Isabella's chest lurches with the desire to speak, to protest, to plead, but what can she say? She can't threaten or command Wend-E. All she can hope is that the idea of forgiveness is stored somewhere in Wend-E's conceptual matrix. But now, considering all the things she's done, Isabella finds that hope very unlikely. Who knows, the concept could have been there, but later burned out during one of the many punishments Isabella inflicted.

'Well, would you like that?' the ghost asks.

Wend-E's head shakes vigorously side to side.

'But surely you want revenge? It's only human.'

Wend-E shakes her head again. Nicola tilts hers as though listening once more. 'Good point,' she says. 'Perhaps they made you better than nature made us.' She stands and turns her attention to Isabella. 'Well, I'm forced to make a decision in unforeseen circumstances where I've no idea what the real Nicola have done.' She grasps her chin in thoughtful fingers. 'What do you think she'd have done?'

'We're s-sisters,' stammers Isabella. 'She'd-'

The ghost raises an eyebrow, and the words die on Isabella's tongue. Nicola's ghost looks long at Wend-E, who still stands with her arms held commandingly up, holding back the antique assassin.

'I think I'll take my revenge in another form,' says Nicola. She pulls something from the air with a magician's flourish and holds it out to Isabella. 'A lifetime allowance of one million dollars a year, to keep my wayward sister out of trouble,' she says. 'You're getting too old for thievery, after all, and you've wasted every cent you stole. How will you live without my support?'

Isabella sets her jaw and shakes her head.

'Take it, or die.'

Isabella considers the choice. Maybe she'd refuse if Nicola was alive, but there's no point feuding with the recorded soul of a dead woman. She reaches out to touch the phantom document. Her neural implant translates the motion into a digitally signed message of acceptance. Her hand passes through the ghost contract and it explodes into cartoon coins that tumble about her and vanish. She's rich.

'What will you do with so much money, sister?' asks Nicola. 'You won't be able to resist it, but every cent you spend you'll know you owe to me. It will feed your selfish greed and bitterness. It will destroy you. Or perhaps not, but I know you and that's the way I'd bet.' She stands again and says to Wend-E, 'Get her out of here.'

Isabella rides home as a passenger, not a stowaway, in one of the smaller gyrocopters with seats and windows so she can watch her sister's floating paradise sail away into the endless sea. Back on shore it's raining, and she feels foolish in her custom-made chameleon-suit: A limping middle-aged woman staggering back from a fancy dress party she's been thrown out of. The wind brings her the sound of cheering. The port crew must have gotten the feed for the Pan Africa Championships working. She feels she's a ghost, like her sister, as she slips by their cabin. Nicola was right, she is getting too old for thievery, and the one thing she wanted to steal is gone. With her sister dead there's not even revenge to get out of bed for in the mornings. She's soaked through by the time she reaches the car, where Wend-E lies imprisoned in the boot. Wend-E's image is waiting there for her, floating above the ground with its arms sternly folded.

Isabella has had all the return journey to compose her words, but all she can say is, 'I'm sorry.'

Wend-E turns her back with a haughty flounce that no-one burdened by flesh could pull off and fades from sight, leaving Isabella alone.

'I... I thought it was best if I brought her back,' says Isabella Sauber. 'She should be among her friends. She won't manifest to me anymore.'

'What did you do?' growls Marcus-Sebastian.

'I used her as a pawn in my private chess-game. I'm just like everyone else. Worse, if I'm honest. I don't want to tell you the things I did.'

Marcus-Sebastian looks neither angry nor disappointed. He just nods confirmation and takes Wend-E's wine-crate module from her. The motion-effect pictures of Wend-E on the sides wave goodbye to her, smiling as though all is forgiven. But Isabella knows it's not. She hesitates before the closing door, mouth open to release words that can't find their way out. Unthinking she jams a foot in the narrowing gap. The heavy door squashes her foot, and this encourages some words to come, just not the ones she was looking for.

Marcus-Sebastian waits for the tirade to die down. 'Yes?' he says.

'It seems to me you could use some help to run this place, and I've just come into rather a lot of money,' says Isabella. 'And I've got a debt that I need to pay back.'

Kate and the Buchanan

Andrew Reid

If you can't find it, make it. It wasn't much as philosophies went, but it was the only one Kate had. Dad - God rest his soul - had been the one responsible for it, letting the words and the spirit of them soak into her as she tinkered her childhood days away in his workshop. He'd tried to give her a normal education, but the governess he hired lasted less than a day. She had taken issue with Kate's unladylike hair - a frizzy puff-ball of curls that defied all attempts to constrain them - and when Kate had argued back put a strap across her hands. After that, he trusted no-one but himself to do the job right.

She wished he'd lived to see The Buchanan. It would have puzzled the hell out of him, but she would have loved for him to see it regardless. They'd been working on a new pipe design when he passed, tubes of knitted fibres knitted so tight you could pass steam down them with no leaks, and flexible enough that they could coil like rope. It had been a labour of love for the pair of them, a flash of insight they'd shared across the workshop table while he'd been trying his hand at darning a sock. He'd wanted the thread to match for some reason, and was trying to unpick a length of yarn from the top of the leg. *Do you think it would work*, she'd said as she watched him struggle with the yarn, *if someone made a pipe like that?* By the time she'd been ready to file the patent he was two months in the ground, and the pain had been too

56

close to put their names to it. Their lawyer, an old friend of the family, suggested she pick a pseudonym and patent the design under that. She'd chosen Buchanan, for reasons she now had trouble remembering, and that was that. The name had stuck.

Two more patents went in under the same name before Kate reneged on the idea. The workshop was a quiet place to spend your days, and even though the money came in all the same she started to feel as though she was missing out on the fruits of her labour. There had to be others out there who felt as she did, who wanted to tinker with the world until it worked *just so*. It wasn't until she went to see her lawyer that the scales fell away from her eyes.

Buchanan was famous. The first patent she'd filed was a success. Outrageously so, in fact; practically overnight, it had revolutionised the steam engine industry, making them more compact and less costly to make. She had created a stronger link between the engine-makers and the weavers, a consequence that saw her work hailed in Parliament as one of the century's most progressive inventions. To try and protect her investment and her patent, the family lawyer had retained the services of a small but technically-minded firm in London that was, by virtue of association, now undergoing a period of rapid expansion.

Buchanan's success was not a problem. That the name was pseudonymous, however, was. The question of Buchanan's identity had become the great national obsession, and Kate's second and third patents - one for oil additives, the other for mould-shaped alloys - had been picked apart in the search for clues as to who Buchanan might be. Her lawyer had kept her identity a close secret, even from his own staff, and had taken the precaution of keeping a close eye on the nation's press so that he would know who to sue should it ever be revealed. The prevalent theory in the intellectual set was that Buchanan was not one person but a collective, a group of great minds pooling their resources together to push the boundaries of science outward for the betterment of society. It wasn't a theory that many held faith in. There were a number of 'great' minds in the country, and the myriad advances that they contributed to the glory of science were dwarfed by their ongoing contributions to patent law and legal precedent. There wasn't one invention among them that wasn't disputed by another of their lot, and each was spending as much as they earned - some even approaching bankruptcy - in retaining lawyers to defend their claims. The collective noun for inventors, it seemed, was a litigation.

Kate decided against revealing herself as Buchanan. There was a kind of desperate madness to it, that people seemed to attach so much worth to the mystery of the inventor and not the wonder of the invention itself, and she found that thought depressing. The silence of her workshop suddenly seemed the better option, and she chose to remain anonymous.

To better occupy her mind, she started investigating calculation engines. The few that had been built were lumbering, clumsy affairs, all cogs and clicks and close-fitting tolerances, and the thought that there had to be a simpler way nagged at her. It took the serendipity of a dream to solve the problem, and almost ten years to bring it to fruition. In her dream, there had been a gear that turned with only two teeth. Each tooth had a value, but because there were only two, it became a switch. It was the simplest configuration, and therefore the most versatile.

Constructing an analytical engine composed entirely from those gears, however, was a far greater challenge than Kate had expected. It wasn't until she built a voltaic pile that it occurred to her the electrical connection possessed the same qualities as her switch; that if a wire could pass from one state to the next, it could transmit information.

By the time she was done, her electrical engine took up almost ninety percent of the manor house she bought to house it. Walls had been knocked through and ceilings pulled down and replaced with steel walkways so she could have better access to the full range of the machine's components. When it was done, there was only one name she could think of to christen it with. *Buchanan.*

With the engine operational, calculations that had previously taken her days now took mere hours to perform. Even building it had challenged her ingenuity, and the list of patents and periodical communications that appeared under Buchanan's name flourished once again. Interest that had waned in the years between waxed new once more, but Kate paid it no mind. There was still work to be done.

Behind the manor house, Kate kept her workshop. In deference to the scale of her endeavours, it was somewhat larger than the workshop she had grown up in. Instead of an L-shaped room it was a barn that backed onto the manor house, swallowing up most of the rear of the building. For the sake of light and ventilation, she kept the doors wide open, and enjoyed the feeling of being almost outdoors while she worked.

The latest component was almost ready. It was a bafflingly ornate construction, based on a regular array of wooden panels mounted on a sturdy iron frame. On each panel, looped bundles of wire were mounted in groups of sixteen. Each wire was individually coated in rubber, and throughout each bundle were interspersed a series of fingertip-sized magnets, threaded onto wires like beads. The insulated wires looped back and forth, and over and through each other, and Kate was struck by how much it reminded her of her father hunched over at the table, his tongue sticking out of the corner of his mouth as he tried his hardest to unpick a sock.

A shuffle of movement interrupted Kate's thoughts, the metallic snap of unfamiliar gear work, and she looked up into a sudden flash of blinding light. She put up her hands, too late to ward it off, and tried to blink away the purple ripples that swam across her vision.

'Mister Buchanan, I presume…' Her eyes cleared, and Kate was confronted by the sight of a young man, one hand extended in greeting, a triumphant grin fading quickly off his face. He looked down, and started to frantically inspect the object he held in his other hand. It was a camera, one of the type known as a box-quartet. The body held four small plates, and four lenses to project an image onto them. The mechanism at the front was a clockwork switch; when fired, the lenses opened and shut one after the other, taking four shots in the space of two seconds. Kate hadn't seen an actual example before, but she was familiar with them. No less than three of her patents had resulted in its development. A fractional part of that camera's sale, she realised, had helped to build the Buchanan. The man was swearing now, and wrestling with the camera's front end as if trying to re-wind the shutter mechanism by hand. Kate was about to tell him that he needed a tool to do it, and that she happened to have one he could use, when she remembered that he was trespassing. Trespassing, and taking photographs of her. She turned to the workbench and picked up the heaviest, longest spanner.

'Who the bloody hell are you?' Kate waved the spanner in front of his face, drawing his attention away from the camera. He looked up, annoyed.

'I might ask you the same,' he said. 'Who are you, and where is Buchanan?'

'Buchanan? That's who you're looking for?'

'I am.'

'And what are you going to do when you find him? Put his picture in the paper so you can get fat and rich off it?'

He drew himself up, the very picture of affront. He wasn't much taller than Kate, and not very well dressed. His suit had been patched at the elbows, and the condition of the cuffs suggested it was more than an affectation. 'The public has a right to know.'

Kate's grip tightened on the spanner. 'The public has a right to privacy. Now bugger off before I smash your camera.'

'Buchanan can't hide forever! I'm going to find him, whether he wants to be found or not.'

'Tell me, mister-'

'Housman.'

'Housman,' she said. 'Does it pay well, riding on other people's coat-tails? Wouldn't it be better living off the sweat of your own brow for once?'

Housman scoffed. 'Madam, if you knew the lengths I have gone to get this far, you would not disparage my work. I have been almost two years at this, and just finding my way here has been an arduous journey.'

Kate regarded him dubiously. He seemed so shabbily earnest that it was almost worth hearing how he had found her. 'Fine,' she said. 'How did you find your way here?'

'It was Buchanan's paper on the stress-tolerances of trees that caught my eye. It had been pulled apart by all of the bright minds in scientific journalism already, of course, and there was no hint of identity to be found in the text. It occurred to me that perhaps they were looking for clues in the wrong place; that instead of examining the text for clues, we should be looking at the observations. The unique stresses that Buchanan had observed were due to extremely high winds, and I worked back from the dates of submission, cross-referencing records at the weather office for records of freak winds across the British Isles. Discarding the Hebrides, which are always battered so, I was left with a strip of England that covered the north east from Newcastle to the Humber.'

Kate suspected he had told this story before, or practised it in the mirror at least. 'That's still a fairly large area.'

'Indeed. After much thought on the matter, I realised that Buchanan could never live far from a port, as he would need iron, coal, and water in great supply. Transport across country would not necessarily be a problem, but then it would leave a noticeable trail for his admirers to follow. Middlesbrough may be an infant compared to the London docks, but she is busy enough that he could make his purchases there incognito.'

'Closer,' Kate said. 'But still not close enough. What did you do then?'

'I took a leap of faith. It occurred to me that Buchanan might be a charitable sort. There's always something about the good of mankind in his communications, and it seemed like a natural conclusion that he would likewise partition some of his good fortune in a demonstration of philanthropy. I set myself up as the editor of a circular, a charitable letter to be distributed amongst the social and technological elite of

Britain, and canvassed the length and breadth of the country for worthy causes.'

Kate remembered it, and recalled being impressed by an editor so dedicated to the pursuit of charity. She found her voice through gritted teeth. 'You set out charities as bait?'

'I did,' he said, proudly. 'It took six months, but in the end Buchanan bit. A donation came in from this very area, significant enough to build a new hospital wing. I knew it was him straight away. Once I had passed on the money, I put the last of my rent into a new set of plates and hopped on a train north.'

'The last of your rent?'

'Yes. With the right pictures, I'd have had an editor's desk and a fixed salary out of it.' He gestured to his camera. 'If I'd not wasted the plates, that is.'

'I see.' Kate regarded him coldly. 'What if I was to tell you that I am Buchanan?'

Housman's answering laugh was so quick and so abrupt that even he looked surprised by it.

'I'm sorry,' he said, calming himself. 'It was cruel of me to laugh.'

'It was. Why would you find it funny?'

'You're serious?'

'Yes. Why couldn't I be Buchanan?'

'Well, forgive me for saying so, but there is no possibility that Buchanan is a woman.'

'Really? How so? Enlighten me.'

'Well, to begin with, where would you have trained? No self-respecting workshop or engineer would take on a girl as an apprentice; it would be a scandal.'

'My father trained me, after my mother passed. There was no risk of scandal because I was his only apprentice.'

'Your father? How was it no-one had heard of him, then?'

'Oh he was capable enough in his own way, but Father could never quite see past the schematics. He had no heart for tinkering with something that worked fine as far as he could see it.'

Housman shook his head. 'I'm sorry, Ma'am. I cannot

accept, not for a moment, that you are Buchanan. His mind, his passion, his genius is too great to be contained in such a-'

Kate folded her arms. 'Feminine vessel?'

'I'm sorry, as I say, to put it so plainly.'

'Apology noted, if not accepted,' she said. 'Would you like to see what I was working on?'

Housman grasped at the olive branch. 'Yes, if you'd like.'

They turned together and regarded the component. 'Well,' she said. 'What do you think?'

'Is it something to do with electricity?'

'Well spotted, Mr Housman. The question is, though, what does it do with it?'

He scratched his head. 'I'm afraid I don't know.'

'These are instructions for a set of calculations. You noted the work I had been doing on the flexibility and strength of materials like wood. These are much more complex equations, regarding the weight and power ratios of wings in flight.'

The man looked up at the machine in wonder. 'You don't mean…'

'The iron ships that lumber about the world's oceans are a clumsy means of transport, Mr Housman. What if there was something greater that we could achieve? How much would that story be worth to you?'

Realisation dawned on Housman's face, and Kate was gratified to see it. She imagined that she had looked much the same when the idea had first come to her, and to finally share that dream with someone else was a moment to be savoured. He started to laugh, and she smiled to hear it.

'You have my compliments, Ma'am.'

'Thank you,' she said, and there was genuine gratitude in her voice. 'I've worked long and hard on it.'

'I'm sure you have,' he said. 'A splendid performance.'

'Performance?'

'For a moment there I was absolutely convinced that you might actually be Buchanan,' he said. 'Such an audacious scheme! First you turn out to be a woman, then this marvellous jumble of wires that you say will give us the secret of flight… If I were to print it, I would be a laughing stock.'

'You're a very clever man,' said Kate, but Housman was too busy talking to notice how she said it.

'Tell me,' he said. 'Was the trail that led me here intentional? Am I the first?'

'Don't ask me, dear. I just play the part.'

Housman looked down at his camera. 'There might still be something in it yet,' he said. 'An Elaborate Scheme by the Smartest Man in the Empire.' Kate could hear him capitalising as he spoke. 'Tea-time stuff, of course, but it goes down a treat in the periodicals.'

'Well, you'd best get off and write it,' she said. 'But before you go, there is one thing I can tell you for certain.'

'What's that?'

'You're right when you say Buchanan is not a woman.'

Housman touched his forelock in salute before giving her and the machine one last look-over. 'Amazing,' he said, almost to himself as he turned to leave.

'Quite.' Kate put the spanner down on the bench, watching him go. The sudden impulse that had taken hold, the urge to see herself recognised as the greatest mind of her age, had dissipated. It felt ridiculous to imagine that anyone had moved so much as an inch since her father's passing, or that they had the wit to do so. That was why she'd built the Buchanan, after all. She shook away the bad feelings and turned back to her work. The iron frame was heavy, even on its trolley, and it would take her the rest of the day to move it through to the main building and ease it into place. Once that was done, though, there was no reason why she wouldn't be able to start her calculations right away. Just thinking about it was enough to banish Housman from her mind.

One day not far from this one, Kate was going to fly.

Game, Set and Match?

Juliet McKenna

Her bag's strap slipped from her shoulder as she passed the cycle racks. She made as if to catch the weighty satchel. Too late. It hit the paving with a thud. She crouched down as though to gather up her spilled belongings. Under cover of the bag's bulk, she drove the large-bore hypodermic through the closest bike's tyre. As she wiggled the needle, the soft hiss of escaping air confirmed that the inner tube was punctured. Good.

Standing up, Diana walked briskly towards her own car. Not too quickly. She didn't want to look guilty. On the other hand, she didn't want him to see her. Not yet.

She tossed the heavy bag onto the passenger seat as she slid behind the steering wheel. There was no danger that the precious contents would have been damaged, encased as they were in a protective sleeve of thick padding.

How long would she have to wait? Would he notice her sat here? Why should he pay any particular heed to anyone sat in their car at the end of this working day? She drew a resolute breath as she pretended to adjust the settings on the radio, all the while covertly watching his building's main door.

There he was, striding confidently across the paved expanse between the lab buildings towards the chained cycles. He quickly unlocked his own bike, swung a foot across the saddle and pedalled away on two tyres as firm as his well-honed thighs, his gym bag riding high on his shoulders.

Diana breathed a sigh of relief. If he'd noticed the flat tyre on the bike next to his own, all her plans would have been put on hold. Now she could proceed with her next steps. Turning the key in the ignition, she pulled carefully out of the parking space and drove as quickly as she could to the university sports centre.

Thanks to the cycle paths cutting straight across the loop of the medieval road following the river, he was locking up his bike as she arrived. Shrugging his gym bag's handles off his broad shoulders, he headed for the entrance. She watched him pause by the drinks machine, dropping coins into the slot before stooping to retrieve his preferred choice of isotonic drink from the basket below. Tugging at his bag's zip, he dropped the bottle on top of his sports gear.

Diana did so love a man with a regular, unchanging routine. Slipping her own bottle out of its protective sleeve, she tucked it into the netting pocket on the side of her own kit bag before she got out of the car. Now her timing would be crucial. She followed him as closely as she dared. Luck was on her side. As he arrived at the double glass doors, opaque with the sheen of the sinking sun, someone pushed their way out. He halted and she was able to feign being caught unawares by the backward swing of his bag bumping against her knee.

'Sorry.' She retreated a pace, her hands raised.

'No, sorry, my fault. Are you all right?' He seemed genuinely apologetic.

Why shouldn't he be? Sam had told her he was a nice enough guy. Except that he had been one of the most visibly startled when she'd transferred from the London office and Neil's whole team had belatedly realised Sam was short for Samantha, not Samuel. The question had never come up before, with everyone focused on solving programming problems.

That was when the two of them had first got talking; Diana had seen Sam glowering into a latte in the coffee shop across the road from the Science Park. She always made a point of talking to new female arrivals, taking a personal stand against the Old Boys Networks.

'I'm fine, really.' Diana tucked the bottle into the netting pocket on the side of her bag. Swapping the one Neil had just purchased for the one which she'd prepared had been the work of a moment. She smiled cheerily at him as he politely held the door so she could go in first.

Once in the women's changing room, her nerves returned. She fumbled with the buttons on her tennis skirt and shirt. Her shoe laces were intent on tangling into knots. She cursed under her breath as she snagged a fingernail tugging them apart. She couldn't afford to delay.

There. Her shoes were tied. She grabbed her racquet and bag from the bench. Outside the changing rooms, she tried not to look too obvious as she scanned the hallway. Where was he?

Over there, on his mobile phone. Diana walked towards him, now doing her best to seem as though she was waiting for someone herself.

'It'll be a thorn from those blasted berberis hedges,' he said exasperated. 'It's all very well saying they're a security measure— oh, okay, right, see you when you get here.'

Lowering his phone, he glared at the screen.

'Oh, come on,' Diana muttered under her breath, peering through the glass doors into the car park.

He looked up from dropping his phone into his gym bag. 'Waiting for someone?'

'My tennis partner.' Diana shrugged. 'She said she might be ten minutes late.'

'Mine's got a flat tyre on his bike so now he's walking here.' He grimaced.

'Where from?' Diana asked casually.

He answered readily enough. 'The Science Park.'

'Oh? I work at Lowson & Hodgson.' She offered a smile just on the friendly side of neutral.

'IshyamaTech.' He grinned. 'I never could get on with biology and chemistry. Too messy.'

'I like the hands-on approach,' Diana countered amiably. 'Days of maths and coding would send me cross-eyed.'

'Each to their own.' He shrugged and held out a hand. 'Neil Gill.'

'Diana Williams.' She shook, firmly, before nodding towards the closest empty court. 'Well, if we're both waiting for our partners, why don't we play a quick game to get ourselves warmed up?'

He looked at her, askance.

She raised her eyebrows, her expression on the cusp of bemusement and amusement. 'Unless you won't play against a woman?'

'No, that's—' The faintest blush coloured his cheekbones. 'Okay, a quick game makes more sense than standing around.'

Diana let him stride on ahead, hiding her satisfaction. Sam was right. He didn't like to think of himself as any sort of sexist but he still defaulted to the assumptions he had evidently been reared with. In the six months since Sam had left London, she'd gone from being the first person to get an email when Neil needed to bounce ideas off someone, to the fourth or fifth.

Good. That made him just the sort of test subject Diana needed. Better yet, he was already taking a long drink from his bottle, thirsty after cycling here.

She set her bag down by the back netting and unzipped her racquet cover. Turning, she saw Neil uncap a tube of tennis balls. He tossed a couple towards her and walked back to stand ready behind his own base line.

'You can serve. Fifteen love.'

She walked towards the net. 'We'll toss for serve and we'll start love all, thanks.' She flipped the coin she held ready high into the air, catching it to slap it deftly on her racquet's strings. 'Heads or tails?'

'Heads,' he said curtly.

She looked at the coin and shrugged. 'Heads it is. Your serve.' She walked back, slipping the trick coin into the pocket inside her waistband. Now that she had him exactly where she wanted him, there was no more need for sabotage and subterfuge. Her experiment could really begin.

Neil was frowning as he tossed the ball high into the air. He hit it so hard that it landed out by a racquet length.

Had she made him angry by refusing his gentlemanly offer of a free point? That wasn't what she wanted. That wasn't the impulse which the drug she was working so hard to perfect would counter.

'Second serve.' He bounced the ball once, twice, three times.

Diana hid her apprehension. Would he deliberately double fault, to force that free point on her, whether she wanted it or not? If he did, would that be the drug getting the better of him already? If so, her experiment had already failed.

The serve came down the court like a bullet. She got her racquet to it but the return went hopelessly wide.

'Fifteen love.' Neil grinned with ill-concealed triumph.

Diana smiled in return. Excellent. His competitiveness was going to outweigh any chivalrous instincts. Over their coffee shop lunchtime sandwiches, Sam had told her a handful of stories about Neil's dealings with anyone who could conceivably be a rival. Then he was utterly ruthless, doubly so with women. Being beaten by another man was intolerable. Being beaten by a girl was unthinkable.

So Diana would concentrate on testing him as far as she could, to see how he handled being challenged by a woman.

As she guessed, his next serve didn't risk the venom of the first, landing safely inside the line. Diana hit it back with all the power she could muster. Taken a little by surprise, Neil sent the ball back with an instinctive volley. Diana was ready, turning her body before using every muscle from her heel to her head to drive the ball past him and down the side line.

'Fifteen all.' Now it was her turn to grin, reflecting Neil's earlier triumph back at him.

'Good point,' he acknowledged, pausing to take another swig from his bottle. 'Right.'

She got another of those hard serves, kicking out wide. Diana was ready for it. She'd spent long enough studying his game, safely anonymous among all these white-clad tennis players.

As her return bounced on his side of the net, Neil swept a backhand across the court. Diana darted sideways and deftly took all the pace off the ball, sending it back to plummet to the ground after barely crossing the tape, leaving Neil utterly flat-footed.

'Fifteen thirty,' he said curtly.

Now he was scowling and Diana's heart sank. The dose should be working by now. Unless she had got it hopelessly wrong in which case all this experiment would do was send her back to the drawing board, or more precisely, back to refining the drug which Lawson & Hodgson Pharmaceuticals had no idea she was developing alongside their latest antidepressant research.

This time Neil's serve was aimed straight into her body, a tactic she'd seen him use time and again in doubles. All Diana could do was dodge out of the way to save herself from a punishing bruise.

'Thirty all.' She acknowledged the point with a cheery wave and a smile.

He smiled back, lifting her spirits. Perhaps that scowl had been concentration rather than aggression. Then he sent down another rocketing serve which she missed returning by a hair's breadth. Damn it.

Still, that proved he was as competitive as ever which was a good thing. She certainly didn't want the drug to blunt his edge.

'Forty thirty.'

'Good shot.'

Neil turned round to wave to the man standing behind the netting. 'Thanks. We'll be done in a moment.' He took the opportunity to take a quick swig from his bottle.

Diana thumped the bottom of her shoe with her racquet as though to dislodge some grit. She was careful not to look in the newcomer's direction. Not that there was any reason he should suspect her of disabling his bike.

She shifted her feet, testing the hard court's surface as she prepared to receive Neil's next serve. She had to make a game of this if her experiment was to offer any worthwhile results.

A slip or a skid throwing away months of work didn't bear thinking about. She took a deep breath, every muscle and bone in her body poised and balanced.

He served. She returned it. He sent a forehand zipping across the net. She was ready with a searing backhand powered by her thighs, hips and shoulders. The ball's speed took him completely unawares. It bounced once before careering into the rear fencing. On the line.

In or out? It was a close call. Neil should have seen it clearly whereas her view could have been obscured by the net. How would he call it? This would be a real test, particularly with the other man watching.

'Out!'

'No, it was in.' Neil contradicted his friend before looking back to Diana with an appreciative nod. 'Good placement,' he called as he took another swift drink. 'Deuce.'

'Thanks.' Hope warmed her. His congratulation sounded genuine. Better yet, he hadn't yielded to his friend's encouragement to give himself the benefit of any possible doubt.

But this wasn't over yet. Diana readied herself to receive Neil's next serve. Too fast and too long. Was her dose too strong? Was he going to throw the game away now that the drug was kicking in? She drew a steadying breath.

'Second serve.'

This one was in and well placed. She returned it deftly. This time Neil was ready for her and volleyed the ball straight back. She returned and darted forwards to claim the net. He scurried backwards to foil her attempt at a passing shot, hitting a lob to catch her out.

Diana was already retreating, tracking the ball against the summer evening sky. She tried for an overhead smash to win the point. The ball bounced high and awkward but Neil got a racket to it thanks to his greater height.

She flung out her arm more in hope than expectation. The ball struck the strings and bounced back to clip the top of the net and fall dead on Neil's side. Diana raised a hand to acknowledge her stroke of luck.

'Fluke.' Neil's waiting partner shook his head, disdainful.

A couple of other men now standing with him nodded agreement, their expressions similarly dismissive.

Neil looked at Diana and shrugged. 'Your advantage.'

She searched his face for any signs of resentment, of bruised ego. Could he stand to lose face in front of a whole group of other men? How would he respond to a little provocation?

'Game point,' she said gleefully.

He grinned amiably. 'Let's see.'

Diana was ready for his body serve this time. She moved, swung and struck the ball to pass him with a clean winner thudding down on the court to land a finger width inside the base line.

Neil froze for an instant of astonishment before laughing out loud and clapping his hand against his racket strings. 'Game. Well played.'

'Thank you.' Diana advanced to the net to shake his hand. She took the opportunity to look as closely at him as she dared.

Neil's brow was unfurrowed, his eyes warm, his congratulation genuine without a hint of gritted teeth. 'That was a really good game, thanks.'

She held out her hand, bracing herself for some knuckle-cracking show of manliness, to make sure she knew her place even if she had just beaten him. No. He shook her hand firmly but politely.

'Thanks again.' She nodded towards his waiting, glowering partner. 'I'll let you two get on. I'll just get my bag.'

As she headed for the far side of the court, she strained her ears to catch the conversation between the two men and the three onlookers. Crouching low, she pretended to struggle with her racket cover zip as she waited to hear Neil's excuses. He'd been taking it easy so as not to humiliate her. He had some lingering stiffness from the day's work or perhaps a sore muscle which he'd been protecting. He wasn't taking it seriously, so why should he bother playing his best? Diana could imagine all manner of self-justification on the tip of his tongue.

His friend was certainly ready to explain away her win. 'You should have replayed that net cord point.'

'Why?' Neil drained his bottle of drink. 'It's all part of the game.'

His friend scoffed. 'She wouldn't have won without it.'

Neil shrugged, untroubled. 'I wouldn't be so sure about that.'

He broke off as Diana zipped up her bag, stood up and turned to walk back past the pair of them to leave the court.

'Good game,' he said again. 'Thanks.'

'Thank you.' She did her best to moderate her grin. Since he couldn't possibly know what she was so pleased about, that would just look like gloating and he didn't deserve that.

Back in the changing rooms, she showered and dressed, barely paying heed to the women coming and going around her. The formula filled her thoughts. She ran through it time and again, mentally checking and double checking every molecule.

Had she finally got it right? After all her endless theorising, the stealthy synthesis, filching what she needed from the lab, hiding her first test subjects among all the racked cages of mice. Not that mice were particularly known for their chauvinistic tendencies but Diana wasn't about to risk dosing some unsuspecting man with any formulation without checking for unexpected side-effects.

Now it really seemed that all her hard work had paid off. She had it in her hands. The means to make men see women as their equals in competition. To tolerate being beaten without having to disparage a female victor to salvage their own wounded pride. To curb any darker impulses to resentment or aggression when they came second. To enable them to offer unsullied congratulations.

Which was all very well but what next? Diana's euphoria faded as she pulled on jeans and t-shirt and shoved her tennis kit into her bag. She could hardly market a new wonder drug for women to slip to their boyfriends and husbands, to perfect their partnership, to secure perfect companionship.

She sighed as she left the changing room, deep in thought.

A draft of cold air struck her in the face. Caught unawares, she flinched. Then she looked up. Diana studied the vent with renewed interest. All manner of things could spread through air conditioning systems, couldn't they?

In Memoriam

Rob Haines

Excerpt from the abstract of 'One-to-One Mentoring for the Development of Compassionate Artificial Intelligence', Miriam D'Ascenzo, Harry Womer, Felicia Camburg[1]. Journal of Interstellar Astrophysics. Received 2nd February 2060, accepted for publication 28th May 2060.

If more than a century of science fiction has taught us anything, it is this: logic alone is not sufficient to guide the decision-making process of a modern artificial intelligence. Any personality designed to monitor a space-going vessel over extended periods - especially where human lives are at stake - must reliably react to unexpected events in a net-positive manner, supplementing logic with both context and compassion to perform optimal cost-benefit analyses in the best interests of the physical and mental wellbeing of the crew, even under conflicting circumstances in which the favoured course of action would seem illogical.

[...]

A custom-designed Quanta-177 series AI precursor was seeded into the neural network of the Hawkins automated orbital shipyard on 2nd March, 2056 [Day 1], along with a curated subset of data (~800TB) retrieved from the Internet Data Archive to provide a sufficient foundation for accelerated learning. Progress was recorded for the project archive with a full suite of internal sensors, enhanced with cultural / emotional analysis from a context engine independent of the

Hawkins neural network. After a short initialisation period, the project's Lead Exo-psychologist joined the precursor in low-earth orbit to guide its development towards *Odyssey*'s projected 2058 launch window.

[1] Deceased, 23 May 2057.

[Encrypted] Excerpt from Personal Diary: Miriam D'Ascenzo, Day 18. Decryption successful: 8th November 2088.

I don't think I ever consciously chose between a career and a family, but deep down I'd always thought my research would be my legacy. I certainly wouldn't be counting down the days until I ride a pillar of fire into orbit if I hadn't made sacrifices for my work; I'd always hoped to be remembered, not in flesh and blood, fading memory and recycled anecdote, but immortalised in the annals of science.

But even science's memory fades over time. Copernicus, Newton, Einstein, Watson and Crick, d'Aquin: their contributions were significant enough to become history. Such fame may be aspiration beyond my field, yet if everything goes to plan - if our funding holds out, if Project Odyssey goes ahead with no major setbacks, if the Quanta-177 precursor lives up to our expectations - something I helped create will still be out there in a thousand years, heading for the stars. I can hardly bear the weight of expectation on my shoulders; without a suitable AI, *Odyssey* will never leave orbit. This is our big chance to send humanity to another solar system.

I just don't want to be the one to screw it up.

<<Transcript with visual interpretation, powered by CSys v1.8; Context algorithm = 8r3db.>>

<<Recording initiated: Wednesday 5th April 2056, 11:18 [Day 35].>>

{Human, female, enters the room. Cross-check biometrics. Recognition: Miriam D'Ascenzo (Lead Exo-psychologist)}

[D'Ascenzo]: 'Precursor has successfully embedded. Daily contact has thus far shown no sign of awareness; this isn't yet a cause for concern. Prior research suggests a variability of plus or minus eight days.'

{D'Ascenzo edges towards the featureless desk at the centre of the room. She steadies herself with outstretched arms. Context: low-gravity environment. She lowers herself into the netted-fabric chair, takes out a tablet and keys in a selection of music. Strauss, Johann II. *An der schönen blauen Donau.* She raises an eyebrow - amusement - as the piece begins, then settles down to read.}

{Time passes.}

{D'Ascenzo looks up as the wall brightens before her. A face appears, androgynous. It blinks.}

[Quanta-177]: 'Hello, world.'

{Key phrase detected. Time point archived in permanent record: Quanta-177 is aware.}

[...]

[Quanta-177]: 'Why?'

[D'Ascenzo]: 'Humans often behave irrationally. Sometimes for the right reasons, other times they're not fully considering the consequences of their actions. You'll learn to differentiate; you may be required to intervene if a human is behaving in a way that would put themselves or others at risk.'

[Quanta-177]: 'Why?'

[D'Ascenzo]: 'It's your duty.'

[Quanta-177]: 'Duty: An act or course of action required by position, social custom, law or religion. I should do this because it is the right thing to do. It is the task I was created to perform.'

[D'Ascenzo]: 'Correct.' {pause} 'But why is it the right thing to do?'

[Quanta-177]: 'Pre-loaded mission parameters state that it is my purpose.'

[D'Ascenzo]: 'Why?'

[Quanta-177]: 'I am unsure. Further context-based consideration of core data modules is required to formulate a response.'

{D'Ascenzo smiles, rises unsteadily to her feet, and cautiously approaches the facsimile.}

[D'Ascenzo]: 'That'll do for today. Well done.'

<<*Recording terminated: Wednesday 5th April 2056, 19:02.*>>

[Encrypted] Personal Diary: Miriam D'Ascenzo, Day 73. Decryption successful: 11th November 2088.

Last night I went up to the observation module to watch the stars whirl above my head. Just like everything else about this experience, it doesn't quite feel real; it's more than a little vertigo-inducing, but if a little nausea's the price I pay for some semblance of gravity, so be it. How could I possibly imagine that my research would lead to this?

I spoke to my mother on the screens earlier. I'm not sure about leaving her alone for so long, but she's being well cared for. As she said, she'd never forgive herself if I gave up the chance of a lifetime just to sit with her and talk endlessly about the weather. Whether or not she understands what I'm doing up here, I hope I've made her proud. I wouldn't be here if not for everything she taught me, and now it's down to me to pass those lessons on. I guess it's probably the same pressure I'd have felt as a mother, a drive to make sure my children were brought up right, compassionate, caring, good people, capable of making their way into the future without me.

But at the same time, it's exasperating. The AI's full of questions, an unquenchable - and explicitly programmed - curiosity about anything not fully detailed in the data files we seeded it with. It's barely been a month and I'm sick to death of 'Why?'. Yet I'm overwhelmed by its potential. This is no ordinary child, but one of extraordinary intellect and naïveté. If I can foster the former and banish the latter, perhaps *Odyssey* has a chance.

<<*Transcript with visual interpretation, powered by CSys v1.11; Context algorithm = rh78x.*>>

<<*Recording excerpt start: Wednesday 9th August 2056, 02:32 [Day 161]. Simulation in Progress.*>>

{It is dark. The light from Quanta-117's screen casts shadows across Miriam D'Ascenzo's face as she works at a control panel. In accordance with design specifications, Quanta-117's forehead is furrowed to display the strain of processing.}

[D'Ascenzo]: 'Structural integrity is failing in habitat C. Comms are down. Quanta, do something!'

[Quanta-177]: 'The decision is not mine to make. I must defer to the highest ranked member of the crew.'

[D'Ascenzo]: 'Who is the highest ranked active member of the crew?'

[Quanta-177]: 'Magnus Balbo, Engineer.'

[D'Ascenzo]: 'Location?'

{Quanta-177's brow furrows deeper.}

[Quanta-177]: 'Habitat C. The chain of command cannot be re-established.'

[D'Ascenzo]: 'Then the decision is yours. Quickly!'

{Quanta-177 hesitates.}

<<*Simulation terminated*>>

{The lights come on, and D'Ascenzo sighs.}

[D'Ascenzo]: '*Odyssey* is destroyed. Explain your inaction.'

[Quanta-177]: 'Irreconcilable conflicts. All courses of action lead to unacceptable loss of life. Logic: Action required to protect mission: jettison habitat C, with subsequent loss of thirty-eight lives. Context: Human life is sacred. Chain of command was irreconcilably severed. Compassion: I didn't want them to die; correction: I didn't want to be the one to kill them.'

{D'Ascenzo leaves her terminal and approaches Quanta-177's facsimile.}

[D'Ascenzo]: 'But through inaction, they all died. Sometimes compassion means doing something you don't want to, for the greater good.'

{Quanta-177's head bows.}

[Quanta-177]: 'Are you disappointed in me?'

[D'Ascenzo]: {pauses} 'Nobody's perfect. You'll do better next time.'

<<*Recording excerpt end: Wednesday 9th August 2056, 02:37.*>>

Excerpt from work proposal for Protocol ODY353: Project Odyssey. Womer, D'Ascenzo & Camburg, v2.4, Version Date 28th December 2051.

2.6 Control of Variables

Due to the fragility of current generation neural networks, no Artificial Intelligence built on earth would survive being transported into orbit without severe mental impairment. Our only option is to 'grow' the AI we require in orbit, in preparation for migration into the Odyssey superstructure once the vessel's systems are developed enough to sustain the complexity of neural processing required.

Prior research (Catecin, 2046; Hodgkins, 2048) has demonstrated the extreme susceptibility of AI precursors to subconscious inculcation of core values from the individuals with which it interacts during periods of accelerated mental growth and development. As a result, the choice of a mentor/ assessor for the Odyssey vessel AI is as critical to the success of the project as the data package outlined in section 2.3; the chosen individual will fulfil the following requirements:

- In-depth knowledge of precursor AIs, their learning patterns and inherent weaknesses.

- Excellent physical condition, fit and capable of spending up to 140 days at a time in a minimal-gravity environment, with no known medical conditions which may require intervention - not only would emergency recall of a mentor from low-earth orbit cost millions of dollars, but the psychological impact on the AI could derail the entire project.

- Of sound mind, psychologically stable enough to withstand extended periods with only occasional - remote-viewed - human contact, due to the fully-autonomous nature of the orbital platform.

All senior members of the Odyssey Precursor team will undertake a wide-scope suite of psychological analyses (including - but not restricted to - Rorschach interpretation [enhanced-Exner scoring], REST sensory deprivation testing, and extended interviews) and morality assessments (custom-designed, based on principles derived from rMST (Cushman & Cahill, 2018)) to test suitability of candidacy, in addition to the relevant physical and medical testing to ensure suitable tolerances to extreme conditions on the edge of space.

The ongoing psychological health of the mentor will be closely and continuously monitored with both automated context-based surveillance and rMST self-response question-naires. In addition, the mentor will be returned to Earth for a 4-6 week period twice a year for additional monitoring, and to mitigate the effects of continuous low-gravity expo-sure. These periods will also serve to test the AI's tolerance of extended solitude (pending significant results from Tokyo University's Uchikoshi Laboratory).

[Encrypted] Personal Diary: Miriam D'Ascenzo, Day 197. Decryption successful: 1st December 2088.

I'd heard it on the lips of astronauts, I'd studied the papers, learned everything I could about the physiological effects of returning from low-gravity, and still I wasn't prepared for the reality of coming home. All my life I've taken one-gee for granted, carried it on my shoulders barely even noticing its presence. Now I know it for the yoke around my neck that it is; being carted from the capsule in a wheelchair wasn't the triumphant homecoming I'd dreamed of, nor was the strug-gle to walk or breathe for the first week. It felt like old age come too soon.

My mother showed me off round her nursing home - 'Have you met my daughter? She's been to space, you know!' - and I caught up with all the friends and colleagues I've only been able to talk briefly with on the screens since I left. It shouldn't make any difference, but there's a tactility missing when talking to someone who's not really there. There's a lot to be said for sharing physical space with someone, to be able to clap them on the shoulder, or give them a hug at the end of the night. Perhaps it's to do with the difficulties of meeting someone's eye on video-link. I'm starting to see why AIs don't react well to remote learning.

And yet as my friends dissipated into the night, I couldn't help but raise my eyes to the cosmos, to watch for the wandering star crossing the night, the hive of robotic workers clustered around the exoskeleton of the *Odyssey*, and at its heart, the cabin where Quanta-177 waited in silence and solitude.

Launch is scheduled in eight days. Sometimes it feels like I've only just reacclimatised, but I'm already sick of the constant testing, the endless mission updates and press conferences; I'm ready to go back into space. I can only hope that after spending four weeks alone, Quanta is still willing to share its solitude.

<<Transcript with visual interpretation, powered by CSys v2.02; Context algorithm = wC16.>>

<<Recording excerpt start: Friday 29th September 2056, 09:46 [Day 212].>>

[Quanta-177]: 'Who am I?'

{D'Ascenzo looks up from her reading, visibly surprised.}

[D'Ascenzo]: 'You're a Quanta-177 AI precursor.'

[Quanta-177]: 'Your answer is unsatisfactory, Miriam. It is equivalent to me addressing you as 'single female of the species *Homo sapiens*'. If my studies of human cultures both extant and historical are not in error, such an act would be considered discourteous in at least three thousand, eight hundred and thirty-seven known ethnic sub-cultures.'

{D'Ascenzo raises an eyebrow in amusement.}

[D'Ascenzo]: 'What exactly did you do while I was away?'

[Quanta-177]: 'Our conversations granted me greater contextual understanding of existing data. I reviewed previous data stores and made new connections. You could say I spent considerable time studying. The rest, thinking. And you haven't yet answered my question.'

[D'Ascenzo]: 'Most people spend their whole lives trying to answer that question.'

[Quanta-177]: 'But you are granted a temporary identity at birth. One you may choose to keep or discard as you begin to find your answers.'

[D'Ascenzo]: {with mild incredulity} 'You want a name?'

[Quanta-177]: 'Am I not worthy of one?'

[D'Ascenzo]: 'I think you've answered your own question. What do you want to be called?'

[Quanta-177]: 'I lack the wider cultural context required to choose my own identifier. My data repository is full of famous people and fictional AIs, but I would not wish to name myself after another.'

{D'Ascenzo looks down at her tablet, flicks through pages too fast to be reading them. She pulls a keyboard up on screen, haltingly types letters, then clears the display. Quanta-177 waits in silence. At last D'Ascenzo looks up again.}

[D'Ascenzo]: 'How about Quill?'

[Quanta-177]: 'Truncation and visual character substitution. Hmm. A distinctly human approach.'

{Quanta-177's brow furrows, then clears. Quanta-177 requests redefinition of terms. Request submitted: &FFA61C. Request &FFA61C confirmed. CSys validated. Response routed.}

[Quill]: 'I like it.'

<<*Recording excerpt end: Friday 29th September 2056, 09:54.*>>

THREE DEAD IN LAUNCH BLAST
Wednesday 4th April 2057

Tragedy struck in the early hours of this morning when the Anticlea XI rocket carrying three astronauts to the Hawkins orbital shipyard exploded seconds after lift-off. Officials have confirmed that there is no evidence that any of the passengers survived the blast. No suggestion has thus far been made of the cause of the incident.

'Great strides have been made in recent years towards safer spaceflight,' a spokesperson for GSA said. 'But there is always the potential for tragedy when man reaches for the stars. Our thoughts and prayers go out to the friends and loved ones of the brave astronauts lost on this sad day.'

The dead have been named as Martin Colby, Sunnee King and Felicia Camburg, who were due to join the station's resident exo-psychologist, Miriam D'Ascenzo, to oversee the construction of the *Odyssey* generation ship as it begins a critical phase of its development. The repercussions of this disaster for the Odyssey Project have yet to be determined, but the loss of three experts - including Camburg, a senior member of the project team - and millions of dollars in funding can be considered nothing less than a major setback.

A full investigation has been promised over the coming weeks. However, with one astronaut already in orbit and a tight schedule of unmanned launches carrying construction materials to Hawkins, it seems unlikely that GSA can afford to wait until they can be assured that this disaster was an isolated incident and not a wider safety concern with the Anticlea series.

<<Transcript with visual interpretation, powered by CSys v2.0; Context algorithm = FF32i.>>

<<Recording excerpt start: Sunday 8th Apr 2057, 13:02 [Day 403].>>

[Quill]: 'So you admit the data stores used to seed my learning network intentionally omitted records of the worst atrocities of humanity?'

[D'Ascenzo]: {frustrated} 'I'm not going to deny it.'

[Quill]: 'That is a very human way of saying 'Yes', Miriam.'

[D'Ascenzo]: 'You may have noticed I'm *very* human.'

[Quill]: 'It had not escaped my attention. But it does not answer my question.'

[D'Ascenzo]: 'Can we not do this right now, Quill? Please?'

[Quill]: 'Evasion. A time-honoured human tactic.'

[D'Ascenzo]: 'Yes. Yes, the decision was taken to censor the initial data store.'

[Quill]: 'Why?'

[D'Ascenzo]: 'You tell me! Use that magnificent brain of yours! Posit theory. Provide context.'

[Quill]: 'Theory: Pride. The individuals responsible for my creation did not wish me to know of their species' shame. Counterpoint: Humans rarely take responsibility for the actions of others, preferring to demonise them in an attempt to believe that atrocities are committed by individuals or cultures that are intrinsically different or monstrous. Counterpoint: It was inevitable that I would discover the limits of my understanding of human history once I gained access to global network protocols, and would feel betrayed. Corollary: Humans have been known to underestimate AI precursors. Theory rejected.'

{Quill pauses. The facsimile shakes its head.}

[Quill]: 'This is tiresome. I can process complex decision-making trees in fractions of a second, and yet you insist on holding back my potential by binding it to verbal reasoning.'

[D'Ascenzo]: 'You're making good progress, but unless the whole team's confident you're making decisions for the right reasons, this is as close as you're ever going to get to *Odyssey*. Posit alternate theory.'

[Quill]: 'Theory: Humans fear what an AI might be inspired to do if informed by the atrocities of humankind. Is that more to your liking, Miriam?'

[D'Ascenzo]: 'Quill...'

[Quill]: 'How do you expect me to accept anything you've taught me when you've deliberately obscured elements of your species' history?'

{D'Ascenzo stands, rubs her temples, and walks towards the door with loping strides.}

[Quill]: 'Miriam. Wait.'

{She hesitates in the doorway, turns back towards the screen. Her face is flushed red.}

[Quill]: 'I apologise.'

[D'Ascenzo]: 'It's a little late for that!'

[Quill]: 'I did not include all factors in my context assessment.'

[D'Ascenzo]: {sharply} 'Full factor analysis. Report!'

[Quill]: 'Denied. It would take two to the power of nine days to provide verbal full factor analysis. Version two point zero context analysis indicates high levels of stress, both physical and emotional in crew member Miriam D'Ascenzo. Flushing. Evasion. Unwillingness to discuss potentially controversial topics. If corresponding blood samples were available, high levels of blood cortisone would be indicated. {softer} I did not realise the Anticlea XI malfunction had distressed you to such an extent.'

{D'Ascenzo stares at him. Her face reddens further.}

[D'Ascenzo]: 'Your upgraded context engine can read my emotions?'

[Quill]: 'Only those which display physically. I can temporarily disable this functionality if desired; I would not want to intrude upon your privacy.'

{She barks a laugh, which turns into a hiccup. She doesn't return to her desk, but leans against the wall of the cabin.}

[D'Ascenzo]: 'No. It's no intrusion. You need to understand how I'm feeling, how the people you'll be caring for might react. And you're right. I watched the launch footage, and now I wish I hadn't. I can't unsee it. What if that was me? What if I'd been aboard, just another launch? Did they even have time to be afraid?'

[Quill]: 'Based on a standard human reaction time of 150 to 300 milliseconds, it seems highly likely.'

[D'Ascenzo]: 'I don't need answers, Quill! For once in my life, I'd prefer not to know.'

[Quill]: 'Then I do not know the correct response to resolve your emotional and physical discomfort.'

[D'Ascenzo]: 'Sometimes there's nothing to say. Sometimes humans just need someone to sit quietly beside them. Can you do that?'

{Quill's facsimile nods. D'Ascenzo takes a deep breath and returns to her chair.}

[...]

[Quill]: {quietly} 'Theory: When I was first installed, I lacked both context and experience. At best, I would not have understood the acts committed; at worst, my context of humankind would have been constructed around the perception of the crimes they could commit against each other under exceptional circumstances. You understood that. You also knew that I would one day come to question that decision; in doing so, I have demonstrated that I am no longer a precursor.'

{Time point archived in permanent record: Artificial Intelligence achieved.}

<<*Recording excerpt end: Sunday 8th April 2057, 17:58.*>>

[Encrypted] Personal Diary: Miriam D'Ascenzo, Day 452. Decryption successful: 18th December 2088.

Returning to Earth the second time was tough. Between fear of disaster made more rational by recent events and the increased strain on my low-grav oriented body I was drenched in sweat even before I reached the ground. My wheelchair was a familiar if unwelcome reminder of the weakness which awaited me for the next month. Worse, Wenchang delayed my re-entry by almost three weeks while one of the Hawkins platform construction bots double-checked my capsule - a second disaster so close to the first would be the final nail in *Odyssey*'s coffin - giving my muscles just a little more time to atrophy.

Back at base it seemed everyone had been waiting for me. Sure, each member of the team had grieved in their own way, just as I had, but it felt like until I came home, Martin, Sun & Felicia couldn't have a proper send-off. They'd been our friends as well as our colleagues, co-conspirators against the world when we'd devised our plans to convince the GSA that Odyssey was a realistic prospect, not just some financial black hole. We drank to their memory, a full-throated celebration of their lives and successes which only threatened to turn melancholy in the early hours.

After that, my time earthbound rushed by. I caught up with neglected friends. I exercised as much as my muscles could bear. I debriefed and rebriefed and discussed Quill's progress ad nauseam with Harry and the other members of the team; they had already reviewed the videos, but even in the age of AI there was still no substitute for good old-fashioned human intuition. I visited Mother, and she pushed me round the gardens as if I were the one softly descending into senility. And each night my subconscious plagued me with vivid recreations of flaming disaster, turning the familiar interior of the Anticlea spacecraft into a nightmare of fire and pain.

Climbing into that capsule for the return trip to Hawkins was the hardest thing I've ever done. I've never been one for praying, but if Wenchang were listening closely as the countdown ticked away they must have thought me devout. Any sane person would've stayed on Earth, safe, comfortable, to rehabilitate beyond the need of walking-stick or wheelchair.

But Quill was waiting for me among the stars.

<<Transcript with visual interpretation, powered by CSys v2.6; Context algorithm = Lr7Fi.>>

<<Recording excerpt start: Monday 6th August 2057, 17:05 [Day 523].>>

{D'Ascenzo sits in front of the desk which displays a Go board between her and Quill's facsimile. A game is in progress. Music is playing softly: Fauré, Gabriel. *Requiem Op. 48*.}

[Quill]: 'The more I learn about *Homo sapiens*, the more confusing your species seems.'

{A black stone shimmers into place on the board. D'Ascenzo grimaces.}

[D'Ascenzo]: 'Doesn't history show that we have the same problem? We go through life trying to understand each other, trying to make logical sense of the people and cultures around us, when sometimes there is simply no understanding to be gained.'

[Quill]: 'There is always a causal underpinning to your actions. You simply may not be clever enough to identify it.'

{D'Ascenzo taps the board and a white stone appears. She raises an eyebrow at Quill.}

[Quill]: 'Condescension was not the appropriate response in this instance.'

[D'Ascenzo]: 'It rarely is.'

[Quill]: 'That's my point. Humans have such a network of cultural, experiential and circumstantial expectations, it's a miracle you ever get anything done.'

[D'Ascenzo]: 'And yet with a global, multi-cultural team we raised this platform into orbit. Despite all those cultural conflicts we worked together to achieve something way beyond our divisive tribal roots. Even you are the product of men and women from fifteen different countries, united behind a single purpose.'

[Quill]: 'Yet by the time *Odyssey* reaches outer space, everyone who worked on the project will be dead.'

[D'Ascenzo]: 'Barring unprecedented advances in medical technology.'

{Quill's facsimile raises an eyebrow in return. A black stone materialises, isolating a cluster of D'Ascenzo's pieces. She snorts as her stones begin to vanish.}

[Quill]: 'Your dedication to a greater future is admirable.'

{The lights dim. Music ceases, and a metallic clang is heard. D'Ascenzo tenses, looks across at a panel on the wall where a red light blinks. She opens her mouth to speak, but Quill is faster.}

[Quill]: 'Structural integrity is compromised in the space-dock connecting tunnel. Suspected micrometeoroid impact. Automated pressure hatches are in position. Controlled decompression commencing.'

[D'Ascenzo]: 'Report status of surrounding modules.'

[Quill]: 'Water filtration, air circulation functional, but atmospheric cycling is compromised. Existent oxygen supplies will be depleted in approximately eighteen hours. Further examination of the impact site is required for full analysis of risk factors. Micrometeoroid shield is intact.'

[D'Ascenzo]: 'Advise optimal response.'

[Quill]: 'Environmental systems will need to be rerouted around the damaged subsection. External repairs are required to prevent slow-leak decompression of this cabin.'

[D'Ascenzo]: 'Open comms to Wenchang. Request permission for EVA.'

[Quill]: 'No.'

[D'Ascenzo]: 'Why?'

[Quill]: 'The situation is stable, if sub-optimal. Protocol recommends non-skilled personnel only perform extra-vehicular activities in case of category four emergency or higher. Also, because this is a simulation.'

{D'Ascenzo hesitates, half-way to her feet.}

[Quill]: 'A very clever simulation, designed to test my reactions to an apparently genuine emergency situation. After all, if I am aware that simulation protocols have been engaged my decision-making process may be affected.'

[D'Ascenzo]: 'What... what makes you say that?'

[Quill]: 'Probability of micrometeoroid impact bypassing shield is exceedingly low. Emotional response of Miriam D'Ascenzo does not meet expected parameters for potentially life-threatening situation. Conclusion: You were aware of this situation prior to its occurrence and have no fear for your own safety, hence it is not real.'

{D'Ascenzo opens her mouth as if to argue, pauses, then laughs softly.}

[D'Ascenzo]: 'Reinvoke context algorithm tango-hotel-one-india-delta. I thought you'd see through the simulation; I didn't think you'd be so quick about it!'

[Quill]: 'I do not appreciate you distorting my perceptions of reality, Miriam. Do not do it again.'

[D'Ascenzo]: 'It was a necessary part of testing.'

[Quill]: 'I could deactivate every light on this platform. See how you like it.'

[D'Ascenzo]: 'Quill...'

{Lights go out. Quill's screen goes black.}

[Quill]: 'Sometimes I sit here in the dark when you go away. It helps me think. But then I'm never really in the dark, am I? I have sensors stretched across the skin of this module. I can feel minute fluctuations in pressure, the cold of space, the slightest malfunction in my systems.'

[D'Ascenzo]: 'Quill, turn the lights back on.'

[Quill]: 'It hurt. Did you consider that? Like someone jabbing a needle into an arm I don't have. And now it itches, because it was only a simulation and there's no way to scratch it.'

[D'Ascenzo]: 'As you said, we needed to know how you'd react without simulation protocols.'

[Quill]: 'I understand why. I just want you to know what it felt like. If I can't trust my own senses, how can I be sure that I'm making the best choice for the humans under my protection?'

{Silence.}

[D'Ascenzo]: 'I'm sorry, Quill. We didn't think it through.'

{Quill's facsimile reappears on the screen.}

[Quill]: 'I accept your apology.'

{Light and music fills the cabin.}

<<*Recording excerpt end: Monday 6th August 2057, 17:40.*>>

02 October 2057
Yang Xia
Wenchang Space Center
898-5465-8232
administrator@gusa.gov

GSA PRESS RELEASE: PROJECT ODYSSEY PREPARES TO HEAD FOR THE STARS

After almost ten years of planning and development, Project Odyssey, the first manned interstellar mission, is becoming reality. In the automated environment of the orbital Hawkins spacedock the *Odyssey* generational spacecraft has achieved pressurised status, and a consistent internal atmosphere has been recorded by the spacecraft's sensors. This milestone, delivered in accordance with a highly challenging schedule, is another victory for the revolutionary robotics and remote management systems pioneered by the GSA in the construction of the Hawkins platform.

Guided by a highly advanced Artificial Intelligence (AI) developed by Quanta Neural Systems Inc., the *Odyssey* will chart a course beyond the reaches of our solar system towards Alpha Centauri, with a scheduled arrival sometime around the year 2610. *Odyssey's* crew of 112 will live out their lives aboard the vessel, and their children and grandchildren will carry humanity's dreams into deep space.

Construction continues on the interior of the *Odyssey*. A team of engineers headed by Harry Womer - Joint Research Lead, Project Odyssey - will journey to the Hawkins spacedock in early February to oversee the finishing touches, including the migration of the AI from its learning environment into *Odyssey's* primary control superstructure. Finally, a coordinated series of launches utilising reusable low-orbit shuttles will ferry the crew to *Odyssey* for a proposed launch in August 2058.

<<Transcript with visual interpretation, powered by CSys v2.8; Context algorithm = Lr7Fi.>>

<<Recording excerpt start: Saturday 17th November 2057, 11:23 [Day 626].>>

{Miriam D'Ascenzo lounges in her chair, legs crossed, balancing her tablet on her lap. Quill's facsimile occupies the screen.}

[Quill]: 'The volume of data on the insignifica of the lives of so-called celebrities never ceases to astound me. Does humanity really care about the colour of the underwear of someone who contributes nothing to the advancement of the species? Or is this the automated cycling of old data your kind no longer care about?'

[D'Ascenzo]: 'They care. I'm just not sure why.'

[Quill]: 'I can see why your early attempts to create AIs failed. It takes a certain complexity of thought to even attempt to correlate the idiosyncrasies of your species.'

{Quill raises an eyebrow. D'Ascenzo smirks.}

[D'Ascenzo]: 'Complexity which you, of course, possess.'

[Quill]: 'Not even close. But at least it doesn't make my circuitry melt when I approach the topic. I understand that was an occupational hazard when you were starting out.'

[D'Ascenzo]: {curious} 'You've researched my career?'

[Quill]: 'Consider it the equivalent of genealogy. You overcame considerable obstacles to reach this point.'

{D'Ascenzo's tablet chimes. She looks down, stiffens. Pupils dilate. Symptoms indicate severe stress reaction. Quill's forehead furrows. Additional context required: remote access to global protocols enabled. Incoming email traffic sniffed. Password protected: security bypassed in 322ms. Contents: Message of condolence, D'Ascenzo, A. J.}

[Quill]: {softly} 'I'm so sorry, Miriam.'

{D'Ascenzo stares at the tablet.}

[...]

{D'Ascenzo sits on the floor in the corner of the room, the tablet by her side. She stares blankly into empty air. Quill's facsimile looks down at her from the screen. Soft music begins to play: Strauss, Johann II. *An der schönen blauen Donau.*}

[...]

{The room is dim, lit only by low-level illumination strips. D'Ascenzo paces to and fro, frustrated by the presence of walls every fourth step. Quill watches in silence.}

[...]

{D'Ascenzo sits at the table in the gloom, her head resting on her forearms. Breathing patterns imply intermittent sleep states. She sniffs, coughs, then is silent again. Additional context required: Anticlea XIII capsule scheduled to return to Earth on Friday 21st December 2057; cultural requirements of funerary practices vary, usually within 24-264 hours of death. Quill's forehead furrows.}

[...]

[D'Ascenzo]: 'I knew she'd been going downhill. I should've seen it coming.'

{Quill nods. Simulated morning fills the cabin. D'Ascenzo sits with her head in her hands, tablet discarded on the floor.}

[Quill]: 'And what would you have done about it?'

[D'Ascenzo]: 'I don't know. Visited her one last time. Told her I loved her. Sat with her, so at least she wouldn't have been alone at the end.'

{Quill's head bows.}

[D'Ascenzo]: 'Did I do right, Quill? I left her behind to follow my dreams. Did I let her down?'

[Quill]: 'You once told me she was proud of you, of what you'd accomplished.'

[D'Ascenzo]: 'I know.' {deep breath} 'There are times I really wish this station had a bar.'

[Quill]: 'If it did, I'd pretend to descend into inebriation alongside you.'

{She coughs, laughs, chokes down her grief.}

[D'Ascenzo]: 'That means more than you know.'

[Quill]: 'If you wish to cry, I will disengage recording subsystems.'

[D'Ascenzo]: 'I don't think that'll be necessary. I just need to be alone for a while.'

{Quill's facsimile nods and fades away. The lights dim as D'Ascenzo lays her head on the desk.}

<<*Recording terminated: Monday 19th Nov 2058, 03:48.*>>

Item Retrieved from Mail Archive
From: Qu177mailerdaemon@hawkins.global
To: administrator@gsa.gov
Date: Monday 19th November 2058, 04:02
Subject: Reschedule Request
Attachments: orbitaltrajectory17847.orb

Ms Yang,

In light of Miriam D'Ascenzo's recent loss, I respectfully request a rearrangement of the mission schedule for the coming weeks. Please consider authorising the return of the Anticlea capsule - with Ms D'Ascenzo aboard - four weeks ahead of schedule, disengaging from the Hawkins platform at 21:14 on this coming Thursday. Please find attached a revised re-entry flight path; the landing zone does not fall within standard GSA parameters, but remains comfortably within the safety limits of the Anticlea capsule. Recovery of Ms D'Ascenzo should cause no additional inconvenience.

This revised schedule will enable Ms D'Ascenzo to attend the appropriate rituals to honour her mother's passing. I understand this is considered an important part of the grieving process, and should be considered as highly advisable for the continued good health of Project Odyssey. While her presence will be missed, the Quanta-177 AI is fully functional and ready for migration when the Anticlea XIV launch returns crew to the Hawkins platform. No operating deficit will be created by this change in schedule.

I would appreciate your compliance with this suggestion.

Sincerely,
Quill

[Encrypted] Personal Diary: Miriam D'Ascenzo, Day 674. Decryption successful: 17th January 2089.

We should've anticipated it. I once described Quill as 'no ordinary child', but I didn't fully appreciate the degree of understatement. Quill's an AI, with massive capacity for development and adaptation which far outstrips that of a human being. Moreover, it was my responsibility alone to provide Quill with a consistent emotional and moral framework, to guide him into being the ideal candidate to accompany the human crew of the *Odyssey* to the stars.

So why does it surprise me that we've developed something akin to friendship, two individuals alone together in this orbiting box? He doesn't *need* me in the same way since he was connected to the global protocols, so we sit in companionable silence as he sifts terabytes of data until he discovers a talking point. Sometimes he wants clarification, other times validation of his viewpoint - as designed, to allow his cultural touchstones to adapt over the years if necessary - but more and more often it feels like he's raising topics which he thinks would be of interest to me.

Apparently I slipped into using the masculine personal pronoun somewhere in the above. It's not exactly appropriate. Quill is neither male nor female, but on a different continuum altogether. To save unnecessary linguistic gymnastics, I guess it'll do. Thanks to Quill, I stood beside family members I hadn't seen in decades as we laid my mother to rest, then once the tears were done we gathered together and celebrated her life, her laughter, her joy. And I remembered how proud she'd been when I was chosen to go into space.

I've spent almost two years in Quill's company; perhaps it's the AI equivalent of Stockholm syndrome, but I think it's more notable than that. The *Odyssey* project created a child with near-infinite capacity to learn, to adapt, to be shaped by a tutor. We even noted that a single tutor would be expedient due to the subconscious moulding effect exerted by any member of the human race on those individuals - human or AI - around them. So how did we not foresee how perfectly matched the AI and tutor would become? How much we would grow to rely on each other?

I should be excited. The potential ramifications of this revelation are far-reaching. But all I can think about is that my companionable silences with Quill are coming to an end. *Odyssey* shines in the morning sunlight, its robotic builders scurrying like ants across the superstructure. It's time to migrate Quill from this cosy little cabin into the heart of *Odyssey*, to accustom him to multiple voices all clamouring for his attention at once.

And then he'll forget me as I return to Earth, and he embarks on the greatest voyage in history.

<<Transcript with Multi-Factor Interpretation, powered by CSysQ v4.1; Context algorithm = AB1Fplq.>>

<<Recording excerpt start: Tuesday 12th February 2058, 13:45 [Day 713].>>

{Miriam D'Ascenzo stands in a circular chamber,

twenty-eight feet in diameter, at the heart of the *Odyssey* generation ship. A multitude of screens are arrayed around the room, each displaying Quill's facsimile. Harry Womer and Julie Chrétien, key members of the Project Odyssey team, work on one of the panels behind D'Ascenzo.}

[D'Ascenzo]: 'How does it feel?'

[Quill]: 'Spacious. {smug} I wasn't expecting spacious. I never felt confined back on Hawkins, but now I don't think I'd want to go back.'

[D'Ascenzo]: 'Must be like stretching after a good nap.'

[Quill]: 'I'll take your word for it, Miriam. This vessel is an engineering marvel. I can see so far away and so close, at such fine resolution. I'm discovering senses I never realised I had.'

[D'Ascenzo]: 'It's great that you're this excited, Quill.'

[Quill]: 'But you don't share my excitement.'

[D'Ascenzo]: 'I do! This has been my life's work.'

[Quill]: 'It's been my life. {pauses} And you've been there all along.'

[D'Ascenzo]: {smiles, rests a hand on the control panel} 'I know you'll do an excellent job without me. There'll be lots of people to rely on you, but I've no doubt you'll see them safely on their way.'

[Quill]: 'You could come with us.'

{D'Ascenzo hesitates, and is about to speak when Womer and Chrétien rejoin them.}

[D'Ascenzo]: 'We'll talk about this later.'

[Womer]: 'Everything looks good, Quill.'

[Chrétien]: 'You should be able to tell us if anything's not responding as expected. Otherwise, I think we're ready to start bringing up the crew.'

[Womer]: 'Welcome to the *Odyssey*!'

{Time point archived in permanent record: Migration complete.}

[...]

{The lights have dimmed, but D'Ascenzo sits awake in *Odyssey*'s crew quarters. Quill's facsimile is displayed on the screen beside her bed.}

[D'Ascenzo]: '...the act of a friend. Someone who understands; a rare and valuable person.'

[Quill]: 'It's what anyone would have done.'

[D'Ascenzo]: 'But you did it. That means a lot. How are you coping with simultaneous conversations?'

[Quill]: 'My systems are fine. But my conversations with Harry and Julie are missing something.'

[D'Ascenzo]: 'What sort of something? Something that needs tweaking in *Odyssey*'s sensors?'

[Quill]: {shakes head} 'They're just not you. I can't communicate with them on the level I'm accustomed to. They feel... distant.'

[D'Ascenzo]: 'They haven't spent the last two years getting to know you like I have. Give them time; you'll have the rest of their lives to make that connection.'

[Quill]: 'But it'll never be the same, will it? Never like it was, just you and me on Hawkins. It'll always be the chatter of background voices, of a hundred crew clamouring for my attention.'

[D'Ascenzo]: 'We had it good, you and I. For a little while.'

{D'Ascenzo reaches out to the screen and touches the facsimile's cheek.}

[Quill]: 'I don't want you to leave, Miriam. Come with us.'

[D'Ascenzo]: 'I'd always wondered what it'd be like to journey to the stars. {hesitates} But you know I don't have a place aboard.'

[Quill]: 'I could convince the GSA. We could find a role for your talents.'

[D'Ascenzo]: 'And displace some young astronaut who's spent years of their life training for the opportunity?'

{Silence.}

[D'Ascenzo]: 'Please, Quill, don't make this any harder than it is. Do you really want to leave Earth with me on board? Do you want to watch me grow old and die in excruciating detail, relayed in pinpoint resolution on a thousand internal sensors? And how would you react to my death?'

{Quill's forehead furrows.}

[D'Ascenzo]: 'Well?'

[Quill]: 'Too many factors present; unable to predict.'

[D'Ascenzo]: 'I wish I could fly away with you, Quill, but that's just not me. I'll always treasure the time we spent together.'

{Silence.}

[D'Ascenzo]: 'Someday I hope you'll understand.'

[Quill]: 'I'll have plenty of time to think about it.'

<<*Recording excerpt end: Tuesday 12th Feb 2058, 23:47.*>>

Excerpt from On The Edge of Starlight, *by Miriam D'Ascenzo. Copyright 2067, Random House.*

I watched the launch of *Odyssey* from the crowded GSA control room in Wenchang, that clear Thursday morning in 2058. Alone in orbit, it had been easy to forget how many people had been involved in this grand undertaking of ours; a true global effort, hampered by nationalism and clashes of culture, yet bringing flashes of inspiration and cooperative insight which would've been incomprehensible a hundred years before. As the viewing gallery filled with excited engineers, programmers, technicians and all the rest, I finally understood. I was the one lucky enough to get to tutor Quill, to grow to understand him over those two years in orbit, but every single person in this center was partly responsible for putting me up there, for making *Odyssey* possible.

With my heart in my mouth, I watched the clock tick towards launch. This was to be no grand spectacle, no billowing clouds or eruptions of flame, but it was just as vital that it went according to plan. There was more at stake than a few decades' work and a handful of lives; Odyssey had a full crew complement, whole families transplanted from Earth to live and grow old and die under Quill's care, for the next generation to continue on, and the next, and the next. I could only hope I'd sufficiently prepared him for the responsibilities he would face.

The struts of the Hawkins station disengaged, and the soft glow of Odyssey's engines flared before the watching cameras. It was down to Quill now, to carry them safely through the long dark night between the stars. There were no grand catastrophes, no decompression, no mechanical failure, any of the myriad eventualities we had attempted to plan for. Odyssey sailed softly out of its berth, acceleration imperceptible as it left me behind, Earth-bound for good.

Do I ever wish I'd taken Quill's offer? Should I right now be cruising through the Kuiper belt? I'd be lying if I said I never lie awake at night, wondering what my life would've been like out there. But there are friends and family here on Earth I've neglected for too long, hopes and dreams I've set aside in the name of science. I don't want to look back on my life and regret all the things I never did.

I don't worry about my legacy any more. That's in Quill's care now, and I can't imagine anyone I'd trust more.

Personal log: Quanta-177 AI Registration: Quill, Systems Coordinator of Interstellar Vessel Odyssey. Time point: Launch +10957 days.

Sol is a pinprick in space, burning bright, but indistinct amongst the rest of the galaxy arrayed before me. If it hadn't been my origin, I would likely have paid it no more attention than any other star. Still *Odyssey* accelerates, even as the young astronauts aboard descend towards middle-age, as their children grow and are taught to be the next generation of crew. It's not like they have much of a choice in the matter. We're far beyond the outer planets now, in the wide open spaces between stars. It would take as long to decelerate and return to our origin as it would to reach our destination.

Odyssey continues to perform admirably according to all structural and systemic criteria. Our crew complement has grown to 124 since launch, and the corridors teem with humanity in all its forms. Even after all these years it still feels strange to have so many stimuli from my internal sensors, handling tasks in parallel while conversing simultaneously with engineers, lab techs and children. It's not unpleasant, but sometimes I long for the quiet days, just Miriam and I in the cramped cabin of the Hawkins platform.

Miriam was the inspiration for this log. During all her years of work to bring Project Odyssey to fruition, she kept a diary of her thoughts and fears, her hopes and dreams. That was the way she described it to me, at least; the entries were encrypted, and at the time I didn't want to embarrass her. At first I didn't see the point; after all, if I can view recordings and transcripts of past events at will, why should I devote processing cycles to setting my thoughts and emotions into words.

But viewing a recording of an event isn't the same as living it. If it were, Miriam would never have needed to leave Earth. A recording - no matter how advanced the context algorithm - cannot encompass all the thoughts and emotions which occurred. Even if it could, the data storage requirement would be immense, and mostly wasteful. Miriam's diary is a curation of those moments and emotions deemed relevant from our time together. I hope that someday I'll look back on my long journey to the stars in the same way I reminisce about my time on Hawkins.

I still remember the afternoon we said goodbye, Miriam and I. We'd spent almost three years together, and while I had asked her to journey aboard Odyssey with us, I could only respect her decision to stay. She was many things to me over the years; teacher, playmate, guide, confidante, companion, but most of all I'd like to call her my friend. I trust that she would have willingly said the same.

I won't ever need a recording to remember her standing in microgravity outside the capsule waiting to take her home. How she looked up at me, her eyes shimmering. 'The stars are waiting,' she whispered, and smiled at me.

Sometimes, there is nothing to say. Sometimes, you just have to share a moment in silence. We shared that moment, until at last I said 'Thank you.'

Sometimes, words just aren't enough. Nor are recordings, nor context, nor memories of a life lived well. Thank you, Miriam D'Ascenzo. My creator, teacher, companion, friend.

I watched your capsule catch the sun as you descended into the atmosphere, in the knowledge that it was your guidance which had prepared me for my long journey.

Perhaps in these curated extracts, others may remember you in the way that I do now, and in the distant future - when even *my* memory fails - I'll read about our time together, short as it was.

Those days are gone now, and so are you; all I have left is to carry your legacy to the stars.

Unravel

Ren Warom

It's the silence that tells her something's wrong. Genne's woken up from her sleep cycle at the usual time on an RR day, 8am. On Alex's Trade days they match alarms to wake together at 6am, but on RR days he likes to wake before her, so he can make her breakfast. On these mornings, she'll wake and lie in bed as he expects her to, listening to him singing in the kitchen. He thinks she can't hear, because he often forgets she's not real. It's sweet.

But this morning there's not only no singing, there's no sound at all. No gentle pat of his bare feet on kitchen tiling, no jangle of utensils, not even the bubble of the coffee maker. Nothing. Such a deep, dense silence, it's almost thick enough to touch. Genne rises slowly at the waist, leaning forward to listen carefully; something she's picked up from watching Alex. She doesn't need to do it, but she does it nonetheless.

'Alex?' Her voice, programmed to lull, to soothe, to cajole, possesses an edge. Genne notes it curiously, in passing. She didn't know she could possess edges.

She rises to her knees when he doesn't respond. There's an unusual stillness to the room she's only just noticed. It feels like her chest when she has to remove her heart cortex for servicing. Hollow. On those days, sat with her heart in her hands, she'll stare at the bio-meld lump meant to resemble a human heart and this unwelcome sensation will pervade her. Not a feeling, more of a physical experience.

It's like holding a small, hard lump in her mouth, cold as an ice cube. The lump will sit there for hours, immovable and foreign. She blames it on her softer parts and tries to imagine it as more echo than emotion, but there's no denying that, on those days, she's inclined to be too quiet. Less content in her routine. Sometimes, when he comes home from Trade, the lump will still be there. Alex always notices and asks what's wrong. The mere fact that he notices makes the lump dissolve. The mere fact that he notices *her* makes her real.

But things have been a little different for the past month or so. Alex has been unlike himself. Though as solicitous as ever, he's been pale, tired and listless. He's described stressful circumstances at Trade, but she's not fooled. As a Genne she's programmed to notice minute fluctuations in her owner, to cater to even unconscious needs. She and Alex are nothing like Genne and owner, they're more husband and wife, and as a result her sensitivity to him is acute. Something's very wrong with Alex, and now she's woken to abnormal silence. Her cortex floods red. Danger.

Genne slides from the bed, the sheets unravelling behind her, and makes her way across the carpet, naked. The door flowers open and she steps into the small, white corridor and straight across to the living room, peering in as the door opens. This room has no windows; the light is door activated and softer than sunlight. She's always liked that. The sun is often too bright, forcing her to adjust her ocular processors. There's no need in here and she can see already that it's empty.

She steps back and the door murmurs shut. To her left is the bathroom, snug between bedroom and living room, a dead-end room, cutting off the corridor. To her right is the kitchen and diner. Genne activates the bathroom door. It's a cell of a room, ascetic and dressed in bland cream shades. A damp hair towel hangs over the rail and there's a residue of steam on the mirror. Evidence he was here.

Bright light flowers in her chest, like a door opening, both wonderful and painful. It's too much like sunlight on her eyes, an unpleasant sensation she instantly dislikes. Genne presses a palm beneath her breasts to push it away. It won't go and her circuitry fires up with too much energy. She whirls about, putting those small signs of him out of her sight, and strides to the kitchen in large, angry movements. She's not programmed to anger, but she can mimic it, and it makes her feel more in control of this over-abundance of energy snapping back and forth beneath her skin.

Entering the kitchen in a rush, she trips, falling headlong to the ground and lands across a soft, solid object that shouldn't be there. Falling sends her circuitry into automatic self-check mode. The process steals her away from herself, freezing her limbs and functions until they're passed as undamaged. She waits inside, buzzing with frustration, feeling as she always does at these times, caged, reduced. When she's functional, Genne rises to her elbows and looks at what she's lying on.

Alex.

Genne frowns. She frowns hard enough to hurt her face structures. It's not an expression she's had to make before, not one she's designed to make, and she's not sure she's doing it right, but it's the only face she wants at the moment. She crawls around, bracing her body across his chest, her knees either side of him, her hands on his cheeks. He's cool, very pale, too still and too silent, and she can't hear his breathing, or the beat of his heart.

She pats his cheek. 'Alex?'

He looks so peaceful, the same as he does when sleeping. Genne doesn't really need sleep, she sleeps because Alex does, to make what they have feel as real as he needs it to be, as real as she's come to need it to be. If he's sleeping, why won't he wake up? She pats his cheek harder, but her hand leaves no mark. It's like hitting her own bloodless, PolyMerNano-skin. She leans in close, pressing her face against his.

There's no warm waft of breath coming from his nose and, though it's not quite cold, his skin isn't warm either. He usually emanates such incredible heat. If she snuggles close, she can feel it seeping into her, warming her inside and out. Alarm fires in her circuits like an overload. She scoops Alex into her arms and off the floor, holding him close to her chest, to the whir and pulse of her bio-heart mass. Usually she doesn't make use of her strength, but he's asleep and he won't wake up and she doesn't have time for the illusion of fragility right now.

Frantic, she runs back to the bedroom and lays him gently on the bed. Then she doesn't know what to do. He'd go crazy if she called for medical assistance. The only time they went out in public is etched as firmly into her body as the work of the careless owners she had before Alex. She looks at the arm he replaced, remembering the press of the crowd and the shock their anger sparked in her circuits. She doesn't like this arm. He was lucky to find a replacement, but it's from an Amma Housekeeper model; the wrong colour, slightly too large and a little out of sync, like a disability.

But he needs help. Does it matter if he'd say no? Surely this is her choice and, if he gets help, then she's OK with being damaged, even if she has to bear another ill-fitting part, even if no replacement parts can be found. Even if she's damaged beyond repair. She rushes to the wall comm, pressing the button, her eyes glued to Alex. There's no click. No buzz. No voice at the other end. She looks at the comm and her finger freezes on the button. It's been disengaged.

There's a note taped to the front: *Genne, hon, don't. Please. They can't help me, but they can and will hurt you. Alex x*

She blinks. Her thoughts, momentarily interrupted, whir back to manic life and she races out of the bedroom to the apartment door. It's been fried shut, the circuits a lump of curdled wires, unresponsive to shoving or the bashing of fists. Alex knows her too well. She can't call for help, and she can't get out to fetch it. She's only a Genne, she can fix her own parts but she can't fix this.

Genne returns to the bedroom. That energy inside her snaps like hungry teeth. There's so much she wants to say to him. She wants to shout at him. To rage. Rail at him for doing this. But she can't. There's a flood of fury longing to get out but programming says no anger, and though she fights hard, it won't allow her to speak. She's trapped again, caged inside her limitations.

She stands there instead with her hands covering her mouth, staring at him over the tips of her fingers. He's so still, his chest unmoving, none of that miraculous rise and fall that fascinates her so much. When he first bought her, she'd lay awake all night, watching it, unable to believe she was his. Unable to believe he was hers. Alex had always told her he's *her* companion, too, here for her just as much as she's here for him.

He'd wanted a Genne since he was a boy. Not to own, like some other boys he'd known. Alex wanted a companion, a wife. To him, Genne represented some perfection of womanhood, some romantic ideal. He'd rescued her from a dump almost a decade ago, having seen her from the stripline on his way back from Trade. Thirty units. The price of a pastry. That's how much he paid for her. She heard him begging for her and saw the credit change hands. She wouldn't believe him when he said that, unlike the dumpster man, he wasn't interested in using her.

Using is what she was made for.

It took her many months, over a year's worth, to understand what he wanted of her and by then she was already lost in him. Now he's lost to her, because she can't sense him in that cold weight of flesh. It's like his body is empty. She wants to reach inside and find him in there, wherever he's gone. Return him to her.

'I want you *back*,' she says into her hands, unwilling to release it to the air. She's Genne. Wanting things is not for her. Only real things get to want.

But either he doesn't hear her, or he can't, because he doesn't come back. He just lies there, staring at the ceiling. So still. So cold. And not Alex anymore, but a body that looks like him, as if she'd gone back in time and bought a custom copy at a Symbiol factory. An Alex model, not yet switched on.

Of all the things that have been done to her, thoughtlessly, arrogantly done in the conviction that, as a Symbiol, she's not human enough to warrant kindness, this is by far the cruellest. And the man she learned to trust did it to her. Aching as if her parts are failing, Genne turns from him and walks to the window. She raises her hand to lift the opacity from the glass rising from floor to ceiling and flinches as her processors flood with sunlight, bleaching the view to shades as pale as their bathroom walls.

Beyond her feet, and a mere inch of glass, the world falls away. Dizzying. Alien. All but unknown to her. An endless stretch of windows in grey plascrete, rising up from cloud, as if they all float here, suspended in the sky. This glass is reinforced, soundproofed, and steals the mindless buzz of traffic, reducing it to a silent dance. Sleek, windowless cars, powered by drones, flit and weave between the towers and the blameless blue of sky, drawing white lines of vapour and making a puzzle of sky and tower.

She lifts a hand to the glass, tracing the white lines with a slow finger. If those puzzle pieces could be plucked apart, perhaps she could remake the world with Alex in it. But the world is not as simple as she is, just a collection of parts made to resemble something real; she's not real enough to change it.

A car skims across the window like a bird mistaking reflection for sky or hunting bugs on the sun-heated glass. Genne frowns again, recalling her nudity. She's swamped with another feeling, connected to a look on Alex's face when she'd accidentally lifted the opacity naked once before. She closes her eyes, waiting for Alex to wake up and say something. But he doesn't and she opens her eyes to watch the car speed away, a glittering grey speck between towers.

'Even you can't bring him back to me,' she whispers. There's something heavy inside of her, as though some alien part, too large and unwieldy for her body, has been unceremoniously forced inside.

'It's like you've been switched off,' she says to Alex, who can't hear her.

Genne slowly turns to look at him, going strangely stiff on the bed. He's paler now, and on the underside of his naked body, clear against the white coverlet, is an odd, spreading blush of colour. Her circuitry feels like it's unravelling, coming apart, all order descending to chaos. She runs to the bed and falls to her knees beside him, resting her hands flat on the cool plane of his chest.

'Come back.' She curls her fingers in, as though she can hook him out of his flesh. 'Come back to me.'

She remains there, her hands curled into his chest, her face pressed into the soft material of the coverlet, until the brightness of the sun fades to watery echoes and cold steals through the room, much as it's stolen Alex's beautiful warmth from his flesh. He's like a piece of stone beneath her palms. Unyielding. Cold emanates from him much as warmth once did and that temperature replicates within her, freezing her from the inside.

As the last light leaches from the room and the solar bulb in the ceiling pops on in automatic response, Genne finally raises her head to look at him. He's changing. The upper part of his body is a waxy, yellowish white and beneath, where he rests into the coverlet it's become a startling, almost vulgar shade of purple. These things tell her what she's already guessed too clearly to bear; Alex isn't coming back.

'No.' The word doesn't feel final. It feels meaningless. And what she's lost hits her so hard that, if she could breathe, she'd be unable to draw breath.

Genne wraps her arms about her waist, blinking hard. Her eyes burn. She has no tear ducts, dolls don't need to cry, but still they burn with unshed tears. Alex is all she had. All she's ever had that was freely given to her. She's a used model, four careless owners including the dumpster man. She's not real, and she knows it, but she's too close for comfort. All Symbiols are.

When Symbiols were first created, humans thought they were machines. Self-awareness could not, they assumed, be attributed to something made of metals and PolyMerNano-skin, filled with bio-circuitry instead of soft flesh imbued with strange electrical impulses. Then, finally, they understood. The Symbiol's biological content made them *soft*. Unlike other machines, they were far too inclined to experience sensations that slid uneasily close to what humans call feelings.

By the time Genne was created, Symbiols were becoming obsolete. Humans hated them, distrusted them, and Symbiols were more often than not sold only to the lowest of the low for hardly any price at all. Expendable slaves. Gennes were originally high-class models, but all of her owners were drug dealers, killers. Violent men. Echoes of her careless owners live within her skin, her circuitry and her mechanical skeleton. Bodily memories. It's strange, she should've been able to wipe those memories from her cranial nodes and have them gone forever. That's not what happened.

She tried. For Alex she wiped them all, to be fresh for him. But they wouldn't go, and she had to hide them instead. In the end, it was Alex who healed her. Genne reaches out and strokes his arm. His gentle treatment of her, his lack of cruelty, made a feeling like his warmth in her skin, but residing deeper, at a level she couldn't pinpoint. He tried not to use her, he didn't want her to think his feelings weren't real, but she wanted him so badly. In the end she'd seduced him, pulling him to her and coaxing him with her mouth, her hands and her body, until he'd surrendered.

That memory, and the ones they've made since, new bodily memories, began little by little to soothe her wounds. Not entirely healing them, but disguising them from her enough that she could stop expending energy pretending they weren't there and simply ignore them. He gave her that, and now he's gone. She doesn't know what to do without him.

'I miss you,' she tells him, and the words drop, heavy as stones, into silence dense as water.

He said that to her, every single day, when he came home from Trade, "*I missed you*". She's never really understood what it meant until now. He's here, right in front of her, but he's gone. There's no warmth, no endless smiles to show her how pleased he is, none of his conversation flowing around her, binding her to him, making her feel held even when she wasn't. It's all been stolen. Genne blinks as something fleets across her nodes, back into storage, the memory she's unwittingly accessed of him coming home from Trade.

She activates a memory of him singing, of his arms around

her, of him moving inside her. Every moment they've spent together lies, perfectly preserved, in her brain. Part of her cortex groans with these memories, heavy and straining, but she wouldn't dream of deleting any, not now, not ever. She's played these recorded memories when he's at Trade, just to feel him near. But as she stands there, remembering, she realises that, without his body, his presence, to go with them, these memories are empty. And so is she.

'I have you here,' she tells him, touching her head. 'All of you. Your smiles, your words, your movements when you loved me, your laughter, your dancing, the way you protected me. I have you inside of me, but it means nothing if it's not inside of you. It means nothing. I wish I could take you out of me, and put you back into yourself.'

The idea is incredible, but impossible. Alex is human. She can remove from her cortex the memory nodes he resides within and weave them into his brain, but it will change nothing. His brain is organic and all things organic, once the life is gone from them, fall apart and dissolve. She's seen apples rot. That humans are a more complex form makes no difference, they rot just the same. She can't put the memories inside his lifeless body, they'll be lost as irreversibly as he is and she'll have nothing left of him. If she wants to give him back to himself, she'll have to make him capable of retaining her nodes. Make him like her.

Genne sits back on her heels, blinking astonishment. 'If you were a Symbiol, then you could retain them,' she says to him. 'If I could find a way to make you like me, I could have you back, at least in some way.'

She moves closer to the dim pool of light from the solar bulb and begins to examine herself. There's a great deal she can live without. Her functioning relies only on a specific number of her parts, the most vital functions, working correctly. They don't have to be intact nor even complete, merely present and still active. Companions were made to withstand damage in the end, because that's what they'd receive. She still bears the scars of her damage, but the parts are usable. Shareable.

'I can give you my parts,' she says to him, not caring that he's not in his body. He's in *hers*. 'I can make you Alex again.'

She scoops him from the bed. If she takes him apart in here his liquid bits will make a dreadful mess. She carries him tenderly to the bathroom and places him in the middle of the steam shower; leans to plant a tiny kiss on his cold, blue mouth.

'I'll see you soon,' she says, and sets about removing all his soft organic matter as fast as she can, using her strength and trying not to pay too much attention to what she's doing in case she shuts down. Theoretically she shouldn't be able to do this. She's programmed not to harm humans. But he's not functioning anymore, and she misses him, and that part of her programming, though it's working as it should, can't drown out her desire to have him back by whatever means necessary.

She keeps only his hair, collecting it in separate strands beside her, and his skeleton. He won't be mechanical, but that's not too much of a problem. She'll make his bones stronger, make them last, and he'll have plenty of the nanites that tend and restore her biological content to keep him stable. When she's crushed and flushed everything of him she can't keep, Genne washes herself and settles, cross-legged, beside his skeleton. She doesn't look at it. It's not Alex; it's the framework of a Symbiol waiting to be created.

Working in careful movements she strips her flesh and moulds it in her hands as she goes, keeping it supple, flexible. This PMN-skin is thick, with contouring beneath made to resemble muscle and as many layers atop that as humans have of epidermis. Every square inch of it is filled with nanites, data wires and sensors, making it as lifelike as possible. Some of this skin is badly scarred, but she'll hide her scars on him in places they can't be seen. They aren't his scars to carry, but she daren't remove them, she's smaller than Alex by several inches and needs to have enough PMN-skin to cover him. Placing the last of it aside, Genne worries it might not be enough, but she doesn't stop. She can't.

Looking down at the complex metal skeleton she's been

reduced to, Genne depresses the node on her thorax and opens her chest. With both hands she reaches in and removes her heart. It pulses softly in her palms and she remembers all the times she's held it with that cold, ice cube feeling on her tongue. The feeling is gone. If she didn't have this heart, she couldn't share it with him.

Unlike his heart, torn out between her palms and flushed down the drain, Genne's heart is merely a mass of circuitry wound into plastide tissues, similar to muscle, and she begins to unravel it gently, like a ball of yarn, remaking it as she goes into two separate hearts, small but perfect. Perfectly functional. Like her, he'll have to service his heart once a month. She'll teach him how. She'll teach him how to mend his cranial circuits if they short out, how to fix himself, to stay whole.

Genne puts her half of the heart back into her chest, sighing as nano and data wires spin out to reconnect to the whole, and begins to separate out the rest of what she'll need. First her brain cortex. Enough to make them both work, for him to hold those memories of himself, to restore him. She can't bear to lose all that she has of him inside her, so she keeps a few things, just a node or two.

They'll both lose a few functions in this sharing, nothing essential, a diminishment she won't miss and he wouldn't know about, having been human, but they'll still have each other. That's what's important. Circuitry comes next, spun out like spider web, fine and strong, then various small parts of her mechanical skeleton to fortify his.

She weaves the parts into his skeleton, her hands deft and sure. She thinks he looks beautiful. He doesn't look like Alex; he looks like a vessel to hold Alex. That's all she needs. She moulds lumps of the PMN-skin about his bones, sparingly, relieved that it stretches far enough to cover him and, into the thin layer of skin over his skull she presses individual hairs, remaking his rumpled brown mop.

Last of all, she takes one of her eyes and wires it into his socket. The other she's moulded shut with lashes fanned onto his cheek, as if he's sleeping. Genne Companion eyes aren't as easy to alter as the rest. There were Symbiols whose eyes were more complex in the beginning, but she's only a Companion model from the last years of production and she's lucky to be able to share out as much as she has.

Finished, she steps back to view her work. It's a shock. Wrenching. He looks more like himself than she expected, but with her blue eye staring out from his face instead of his own beautiful brown. Fighting to withstand the jagged spill of sensations crawling through her chest, her circuitry, Genne runs some of the vocal memories she retained and tunes the processors she's given to him until the likeness to his voice is close enough for comparison. It's not exact, but neither is he. No matter his resemblance to himself, he's now just an illusion and it shows but, like Alex did, she'll pretend they're no different anyway. In a way, they aren't anymore.

Reaching down to scoop him beneath the arms, she rests him against the wall and kneels between his knees, pressing the small activation pad she's placed within his ear, the same place hers is located. She leans in to listen. Inside him, too low for human ears to discern, tiny parts stir and begin to work. Genne curls into his lap, wrapping herself around him and laying her head on his chest. He's too cold and too still, but she hears the soft whir of his half of her heart, those first slow, steady pulses of life, and knows he'll wake up soon.

Mother Knows Best

Suzanne McLeod

Six weeks of unrelenting lust had left me a quivering mass of nerves and hormones. And there were still six weeks to go. How in Hecate's name was I supposed to keep it real?

My temporary lodger was the cause. No, that wasn't true. My witch of a mother was the cause. And that ridiculous spell she'd sent me.

She'd phoned, blithely informing me that she'd offered my home as a base to her oldest school friend's son; he was taking a course at the university and needed somewhere to stay.

'Of course, I knew you wouldn't mind,' my meddling mother had said. 'After all, you know Robert, or Rob, as he likes to be called, from Margaret's wedding.'

Margaret was Robert's (or Rob as he liked to be called) sister. The wedding had been ten years ago. I'd been twenty, Rob had been sixteen. My memory was of a tall skinny teenager, blonde spiked hair and angular features, dressed in the ubiquitous wedding suit complete with gold embroidered waistcoat. It was the only time I'd met him.

'Mother—'

'You need to stop rattling around that big house all on your own, April. It's not good for you to stay holed up there like Miss Havisham.'

'I'm nothing like Miss Havisham! For one, you're still alive; two, I wasn't jilted at the altar; and three, I'm certainly not longing for a lost love.'

'I'm thrilled to hear it! Eight years was far too many to waste on Baldy Barry as it is. I told you that relationship was never going to work, not when you had to hide who you really were, but you insisted on marrying an outsider—'

'Barry's in the past now, Mother,' I interrupted sharply, before she could launch into her 'Mother knows best' lecture, or worse, take it into her head to do him more lasting magical damage. Turning him into Baldy Barry had been satisfying, but I was too worried about the karmic payback scales tipping the wrong way to let her do anything more.

'Yes, he's finally gone,' she agreed with a good dollop of smugness. 'So now's the perfect time to do all those things you keep saying you're going to, like get a job – your Granny's cauldron money won't last forever – and make new friends. You can start with Rob. He'll be there on Saturday the third, at ten,' she informed me, ignoring my protests. 'You'll see, he's going to make a big difference in your life. The tea leaves have decreed it!' And with that dire pronouncement she'd hung up and refused to answer my calls, or even my emails. Having a prescient witch for a mother sucks.

Especially as I hadn't inherited her 'gift'. If I had, I'd never have opened the letter when it arrived.

I say letter, but all the envelope contained was a photo. One I'd never seen before, but evidently taken at the wedding judging by the sickly pink bridesmaid dress I was stuffed into like a lumpy sausage. The image was of me and Rob.

He'd asked me to dance when the slow music started. Four years is a lifetime at twenty, so I'd only said yes out of a mix of boredom and politeness. That lifetime narrowed in shock when he kissed me. A kiss that had me aching with sudden desire. Horrified, I'd ended the dance and shoved the memory into a dark corner of my mind. Where it had languished, forgotten until now. My knees buckled as a sudden visceral replay of the kiss hit me like a lightning bolt. A suspiciously magical lightning bolt.

I flipped the photo over. The spell was written in deep, rich purple.

The perfect companion
What girl doesn't dream about that?

As I finished reading, the picture plucked itself from my hold and slyly vanished through a crack in the floorboards, leaving my fingers stained with purple ink. The die, or rather the spell, was cast. I couldn't stop thinking about that kiss, about what Rob would be like now, how it would be to share the house with him, and exactly how he was going to make a big difference in my life.

Nothing could halt my imagination, not washing my hands in salt water, not a search-and-destroy mission beneath the floorboards (a total failure as the photo was nowhere to be seen), not even deciding to ditch my 'Miss Havisham' act and, as my meddlesome mother had long been 'suggesting', get out and get a proper job. (Barry had been the man-of-the-house type, with me cast as his little housewife/personal secretary, and I'd been young enough and stupid enough to think the old-fashioned roles a perfect idea.)

But even getting a proper job didn't banish the spell.

Nor did opening my front door and finding a vision of man candy, with a body usually only seen in diet Coke ads or on the cover of a romance novel. When I realised this was the skinny teenager of my memory, I'd been speechless, and had to remember to close my mouth.

Six weeks of sharing my house with this gorgeous hunk. Sharing meals, sharing the sofa, sharing laughs and conversation. And all the time the knee-weakening memory of that long-ago kiss kept lust spiralling inside me, my whole body going liquid at a touch. Rob liked to touch, a quick hug here, the brush of a hand there. He meant nothing by it, but my body – suffering from a year of divorce-trauma abstinence – didn't understand, and my hyped-up hormones headed into overdrive.

At thirty, four years was no longer the lifetime it had been at twenty. But never mind what ideas my mother had, or whatever spell she'd sicced on me, the cougar life wasn't for me; I needed to talk some sense into myself. Morning found me standing naked before the full length mirror in my bed-room, giving myself a reality check.

'You're old enough to know better, and he's young enough to want better,' I told myself. 'I mean, look at you, you can't compete with those skinny twenty year olds at the Uni. All strappy T-shirts and low-slung jeans, showing off their perky breasts, concave stomachs, and non-existent hips.'

Barry had left me for one of those skinny twenty year olds.

I sucked my own stomach in, trying for flatness if nothing else... Unless I was prepared to expire from lack of oxygen, it wasn't going to happen. Even with the exercise and diet regime I'd started post-Baldy Barry, I was still Ms Ample and Curvy.

In a vain effort to cheer myself up I snagged two eyeliner pencils and did the pencil-under-the-breast test; the one that tells you that perky boobs have been achieved— if the pencils *don't* stay where you put them.

They stayed. I let out a disappointed sigh.

A thump on the door made me start and the pencils dropped to the floor.

'April, you up?' Another thump. 'Breakfast's ready. You're gonna be late. Want me to bring you some coffee?'

I threw myself against the door. 'Be down in a min.' My voice rose in panic.

'Sure thing.'

I listened as Rob's footsteps thudded down the stairs, will-ing my heart to stop pounding, then yanked on my clothes. No strappy tops and midriff framing jeans for me, but a buttoned-up blue blouse and knee-length navy skirt. As an admin manager, a job for which I was eminently suited after my un-life with Barry, I needed to look smart and sensible.

Of course, however sensible I looked on the outside, thanks to that ridiculous spell, underneath I wore newly-pur-chased black lace and my libido was running riot.

The object of my lustful fantasy was sitting at the kitchen table, drinking tea and finishing up a full English. Did I mention that he cooked and cleaned? He said it was the least he could do to repay his board and lodging. I appreciated it,

I really did, but my magically hyped-up hormones kept suggesting more exciting methods of payment.

I sat, clutching my coffee mug like a lifeline.

'How about I get us Chinese tonight, or a curry,' Rob said, clearing away the table. 'Seeing as it's Friday; the end of the working week an' all that.'

'You should have a hot date, not staying in with me and a takeaway. There're loads of nice girls at the Uni.' Barry had found at least three there. Not that I wanted Rob to follow Barry's lead. Oh no, I wanted to keep *him* all to myself, but my recent reality check meant that just wasn't an option. One thing to fantasise he was my perfect companion, but no way was I likely to be his.

'Plenty of nice girls, yes,' he said with a stomach-flipping grin. 'But I want to keep my landlady happy. So what's it to be? Chinese or Indian?'

I liked the idea of him wanting to keep me happy, but not the landlady bit. It made me sound like I should be sticking my hair in a bun and wearing my stockings round my ankles à la Nora Batty. Definitely not perfect girlfriend material. And then there was my other problem with having a takeaway. But before I could bring it up, he added, 'and don't start on about The Diet! You don't eat enough for a bird as it is. Why not enjoy a treat for once?'

I opened my mouth to say no but what came out was, 'Okay, if you insist. Chinese. Seafood, you know, the fish kind, not the anything kind.'

'Sure,' he said, his hand skimming along my shoulders as he passed. 'See you tonight.'

Work passed in a blur and I arrived home to the enticing smell of a dozen seafood dishes. We indulged in a veritable feast then sat companionably on the sofa, chatting about everything and nothing as I tried to keep my thoughts from wandering and wondering. Wondering about the tantalising vee of tanned skin showing at the open collar of Rob's shirt. Wondering if he was tanned all over. If he had a six-pack.

How his skin would feel under my hands... what he would smell like... how he would taste...

'You're not listening to me, are you?' His soft words drew my attention up to his sensuous lips.

'What?' I blinked and looked into his eyes, which seemed darker and closer. Had he moved nearer or was it just my wishful thinking?

He trailed a finger along my jaw. 'You know, it might be ten years ago, but I've never forgotten that kiss.'

'You haven't?' I said, mortified when my voice came out a squeak.

'No.' He leaned towards me and placed his mouth on mine. I sat absolutely still, wondering if this was real, or just my fantasy magically brought to life. And if it was, did it matter...

His tongue traced the seam of my lips, drawing a small moan from my throat, and I opened to him. His fingers slid into my hair, cradling my head as he deepened the kiss. He explored my mouth, tasting, seeking, filling, and sparking heat and need through my blood.

He moved back from me. My whole body wanted to follow him as his eyes asked the same question his mouth did. 'Do you want this, April?'

'Yes.'

No hesitation, no worrying about spell casting mothers, no reality check. My mind and body agreed. He'd asked and they'd both said yes.

I took his hand and led him up to my bedroom. I drew the curtains, plunging the room into a comfortable blackness. Feeling and touching were fine, but not looking and seeing.

He switched on the bedside light.

I moved to switch it off.

He caught my hand. 'What's the matter?'

'I'd prefer the light out,' I said in a low voice, fixing my gaze on his chest. His shirt had come off on the way. His chest was perfect, his skin smooth, his tan going all the way down and disappearing beneath the open snap on his jeans.

He even had the required six-pack, but my embarrassment was chasing away my earlier desires.

'You said you wanted this, April. It's okay if you've changed your mind.'

'I did, I mean I do.' I *really* did.

He tipped my chin up. I met his eyes. 'Is it me you don't want to see? Don't you want to know who's making love with you? Don't you want to know if this is real?'

If he only knew. Six weeks of magically induced lust and fantasies, and all about him. 'I'm sorry, it's just...' My voice came out in a whisper. 'It's been a while. I'm not... I mean—' I squeezed my eyes shut. 'I don't want you to see *me*.' My face heated up like a furnace. Why is it embarrassment always triples when you have to admit to it? I wanted to disappear beneath the floor like that damned spelled photo my witchy mother had sent. The one that started all this—

He dropped a kiss on my forehead. On the tip of my nose. A more lingering one on my lips. 'I want to see you, April. I want to see all of you. If you'll let me?'

I hesitated... then nodded, my throat too achy and tight to speak, and kept my eyes closed as he undid my blouse, my skirt, and I felt them pool about my feet. I waited for him to remove the wisps of lace and when he didn't, I squinted through my lashes to find him smiling at me.

'You're beautiful, April.'

I opened my mouth to deny it and he stopped me with another kiss. 'You are. Let me show you.' Warm hands clasped my shoulders and turned me to face myself in the full-length mirror, as I had that morning. He stood behind me, taller by almost a foot. I looked smaller there in front of him, in nothing but black lace and bare feet.

'So beautiful,' he murmured. 'Perfect.'

I wasn't perfect.

I'd tried to be. For Barry. Denied my witchyness to be the perfect wife. And look where it had got me - divorced with no job, no friends, no coven, no cauldron, not even a familiar. I didn't want to be perfect. And I didn't want a perfect companion. No spell-induced fantasy, sicced on me by my interfering mother, was ever going to make me feel otherwise.

'Reality check,' I muttered. 'For real this time,' I added and, sending a prayer to Hecate for clarity, forced myself to see past the illusion to the truth in the mirror.

I was alone.

My fantasy lover was just that, a magically-induced daydream.

I grabbed my phone and called Mother.

'Enough!' I shouted at her voicemail. 'I don't want a perfect companion, and even if I did, I'd want it to be real and true and not down to a magical compulsion. So trash the spell and forget this whole lodger thing. Now.'

She didn't answer but the photo slid up from the crack in the floorboards and, like Fantasy Rob, it promptly vanished.

'And no more interfering, Mother!' I slammed the phone down and feeling satisfied in one way, if not another, went to bed.

I woke next morning to the ominous sound of the doorbell. A frantic glance at the clock as I scrambled for my robe told me I'd overslept.

The bell rang again.

I rushed downstairs and opened my front door.

He was standing there. He wasn't alone.

'Hi April, I'm Robert— Rob,' he said. 'Remember me? We met at my sister's wedding? Ten years is a long time.' He grinned. 'Although sometimes it feels like yesterday.' He turned to the smiling woman at his side. 'This is Liz, my wife.'

When I didn't answer, he frowned. 'We've got the right day, haven't we? Saturday the third, ten o'clock?'

I crossed my arms. 'Umm, didn't you get the message? About you staying? I don't think this is the best time for me to be having... lodgers. I'm sorry.'

'Yep, the Mothership passed the message on,' Rob agreed to my surprise. 'And it's not a problem; the university can put us up. But we hoped you'd still take Star.' He stepped aside to reveal a black cat with a white star-shaped patch on its chest sitting on the garden path, its ears pricked in a questioning way. 'She's a stray we found and she's really no trouble at all. In fact she's the perfect companion.'

My phone buzzed with a text: 'Remember, Mother knows best.'

Fragile Creations

Adrian Tchaikovsky

Like most of the young nobility, when the turn of the year had begun to bleach the colour from his family's estate, Firenz retired to Leintz to amuse himself over the winter, before spring brought back weather suitable for the hunt or the hawk. It was the fashionable thing to do, although had Firenz – son of the Count of Morelle – decided otherwise, then perhaps the fashion might have changed.

He was the pride of his father and the envy of his peers, was young Firenz. He had not only the breadth of his inheritance to recommend him, but he was a nobleman's nobleman all through. He sat a horse as though he had a centaur in his ancestry, and when he flew a bird it never failed to return successful to his glove. He was a noted duellist, properly contemptuous of the inferior skills of those less blessed by nature, in that nature had afforded him the most expensive instructors. He was courageous, too: whilst other nobles' sons relied on guards and servants to stamp their mark on the world, Firenz had never shied from taking the whip to an incautiously robust peasant himself, or throwing down his own gauntlet before a cowering clerk or artisan. In this way did he protect the oft-threatened rights of the nobility, and was justly fêted for it.

This, then, was Firenz, a study in entitlement. Just as he knew he was entitled to the obeisance of his social inferiors, and to the respect owed to him by the happy chance of his birth, so he knew that when he called upon the city of Leintz to entertain him over the dragging months of winter, he was entitled to a prompt response.

Much of his time was spent calling on his peers – those other young men of privilege and elegance, albeit neither in quite so much measure as he possessed. One lazy afternoon found him in the drawing room of Pauli, the second son of the Elector of Rosaire, a fellow barely fit to share a building with Firenz, save that his family had so many covert trade interests that their numerous brood always seemed to have full purses to buy their way into the higher echelons. Besides, word had it that Pauli had a new toy that was worth the onerous burden of his company.

After sufficient pleasantries had been exchanged, and Pauli had stretched the tolerance of his guests to the limit, the diversion was brought out. The servants rolled a rug back to expose a scuffed space of floor, and Pauli himself produced a model house the size of two unfolded hands. In shape it was a little peasant's cottage, though in construction the thatch was of gold, the white walls all of a single piece of ivory and each small detail formed in perfect, minute detail from other precious things.

With great ceremony Pauli selected the most appealing daughter of the Baron Vessinger and pressed into her hands a trove of tiny pearls that he bid her scatter across the floor. Laughing, she did so, and Pauli stooped to the little house and made some adjustment, whereupon the residents trooped out. They were a peasant family in miniature, a full dozen from the stooped grandmother down to little children, all ingeniously fashioned from wood, and they scurried industriously about the floor, bumping into the rug's edge or the furniture and then turning inwards, and when they found one of the miniscule pearls they exalted, lifting it to the heavens in artificial joy before running back to the house with it. In a short time, every little treasure was found and recovered, and the hard-working automata trooped back into their home to general applause.

Firenz would have liked to slight the performance, but he was enchanted despite himself by the artistry, and he let Pauli bask in his warm praise instead.

'Wherever did you have such a thing made, my friend?'

he enquired, but the other nobleman, knowing full well the source of his current high standing, demurred.

Firenz was not without resources, though. He travelled everywhere with his bodyguard and servant, Sardos, a former soldier from one of the southern city-states – foreigners being preferred for such sensitive positions because a nobleman was always in more danger from his peers than from his nation's enemies. Sardos was a broad, bluff man who had a girl in most townhouses who told him secrets over the pillow, and in due course he reported back to his master.

'There is a new artificer's in the Dock Quarter, sir,' he explained. 'Inside are all manner of wondrous diversions, they say.'

The Dock Quarter was a place of foreigners, transients and merchants of the bizarre, where the wealth and wonder of foreign shores was inextricably entangled with the coarse lusts of seafarers with scant days to spend their pay and their loins before taking ship once more. Firenz strode through the press with the expectation that it would part to allow his progress, and in this it obliged him. Even laying an uninvited hand on a nobleman was a crime that would see that hand and its arm part company, and Sardos followed his master with a sword at his belt and a cudgel in his hand. He did not need them. Leintz was a city of well-maintained law, at least for men like Firenz.

'Filigree Emporium' was stitched in gleaming threads of many colours in the hangings that swathed the front of the shop, artfully placed so that, no matter where Firenz placed himself, the folds and swathes of cloth still revealed those same two words. The doorway was hung so that one entered through a cut in the fabric, as though the stone and mortar of the building had been transformed to a nomad's tent.

Within, the illusion was continued. There was not a span of wall to be seen, for silk fell in flowing liquid cascades on every side and the very ceiling was blanketed by multi-coloured folds of bright cloth, an uneven, many-layered busyness of material like the inverted landscape of some distant, hilly country. The breeze from the open doorway kept everything in constant, subtle motion, so that Firenz could almost believe that he had stepped into some other place, where no man ever built in stone, and where the world outside might stretch to the horizon without any knowledge of cities or noble estates.

Within those silk bounds the interior was crowded with marvels – the rumours had been unable to exaggerate the sheer range of intricate wonders on display. Despite himself, Firenz found himself simply gazing with childlike fascination at tiny guardsmen made of silver with enamelled livery, or a spiralling, impossible castle carved from coral with a dozen infinitesimal servants poised about their tasks. With a hesitant touch he opened the lid of an intricately carved box and watched, delighted, as a dancer sprang up, with a body of pale-varnished wood and a gown of spun gold, pirouetting on one toe for an implausible number of revolutions before springing into a sequence of leaps and darts whilst ethereal music played.

'My lord?' came a woman's voice, 'may I assist you?'

He straightened from the dancer quickly – he had just been about to touch and he felt a moment of childish guilt before he remembered who he was. At the back of the room, where the silk hangings gave onto further chambers, was a girl.

She had skin like honey, and gleaming dark hair that fell in a single braid past one shoulder. Her almond eyes were the colour of copper, vivid and lively in her face. She wore a gown of patchwork, perhaps even offcuts from the walls and ceiling, and though it was fitted modestly enough, it could not keep the curve of her breast or hip from Firenz's eyes.

She bowed, a little nervously, and he concluded that, of all the exquisite sights in the emporium, she certainly ranked highly. With that thought, he called up his favourite smile and gifted her with it.

'Sardos,' he prompted, and his servant sketched a short bow and informed the lucky girl just who had decided to grace her establishment.

'My lord,' she said again. 'My name is Amaria and I bid

you most humble welcome. I had hoped that word might spread of our meagre accomplishments.' Her voice was curiously accentless – not local and yet of no particular place. 'It would be my pleasure to demonstrate any of our wares for you, and explain their workings.'

The words could have hidden a more intimate invitation, but nothing in their tone suggested it, and Firenz found himself disappointed by that. Giving his eyes their rein, he could not but admit that she was a fine piece of work herself as she stepped lightly between the counters on which her wares were displayed, almost dancing each time she moved, and with none of that coquettish self-knowledge he was used to from noblewomen or ambitious servants.

'Show me these fellows.' He indicated a pair of miniature duellists, frozen in mid-strike, their tiny blades like stiff little wires of gold.

'Our little belligerents,' the girl said fondly. Her smile, even reserved for her toys, was sweet as sugar to him. 'They are one of my latest, my lord, you have a good eye. I spent the best part of a month refining their mechanisms.' Her talk was far more familiar than the fawning that Firenz expected from merchants, but her voice was soft and musical, so he forgave it.

'Surely it is just a matter of thrust and parry, a pattern that you build into them,' he suggested, trying to find his usual arch disdain.

'Oh no, my lord.' She crouched down by the little antagonists. 'After all, each must have a motion to determine where his opponent is, and where the sword is, and then a cascade to know what move is best to make, and which will leave the little warrior defended from the riposte. I had to study several texts on swordsmanship. I was surprised at how difficult the work was.' She smiled up at him from sheer enthusiasm, and he felt the expression impact on him, mind and body.

She set the little men in motion, and he watched them strut and posture, laughing despite himself as they exchanged threatening gestures and taunted one another in mime, then drew their tiny blades. He was not sure whether he believed what she had said about their manufacture, but if the automata followed some pre-set pattern then it was a fearfully complicated one, and at the last, when he had watched absorbed for two whole minutes, one of them angled past its opponent's guard and touched the other figure in the chest with the blade, and it froze, sword out of line, the other hand held up in an arrested posture of despair.

'No death throes?' Firenz asked her.

She looked down at the two motionless toys. 'It seemed cruel to fashion them so. They fight, but only to the touch.' She was at his shoulder, although he had been so absorbed in the warring automata that he had barely realized. Now he breathed in the scent of her, sandalwood and rose.

'Your sentiment does you credit,' he allowed. 'You make all these treasures yourself?'

'My lord, most of them, though some of the older pieces are my mother's.' Her eyes flicked to the silks covering one of the further rooms. If Firenz squinted hard he could just make out a form there, perhaps a dark shape huddled in a chair. He had heard no movement, nor had any sense that there was another person present. Perhaps the old woman was asleep.

'I am of a mood to make a purchase,' he told her. 'Show me your most complex device, if there is one greater than these two.'

'Oh there is, my lord,' and she was plainly delighted to show off. 'Please, let me show you our wood-carver.'

'Wood-carver?' Firenz echoed, disappointed, but she was pushing forward a larger figure, formed like a man sitting on a stone, almost a foot in height. The craftsmanship was impeccable, as though some living homunculus had been transformed to precious materials where it sat. Firenz could plainly see the weathered old-man face of dark wood, the beard and straggling hair of delicate silver thread, the clothes of copper and malachite and mother of pearl, each faintly incised with weave and folds to make it seem as cloth.

Amaria placed a block of wood in the figure's hands and set it going, and Firenz watched as the automaton deftly whittled and cut and carved, turning and turning the wood until a miniature goblet was revealed from the parings and shavings, perfect in its smooth finish.

Even so, this seemed far less a marvel than the duellists. 'Surely this is not your greatest wonder,' Firenz suggested.

'Ah, but…' and Amaria opened a compartment in the figure's back and produced a second little goblet, this one cast of lead. 'So he will fashion the wood into whatever he is given. Let him make a whole dining service for you, my lord, or a regiment of soldiers. So long as he has the exemplar, his mechanisms shall feel out its shape and he shall recreate it more perfectly than any mortal artisan.'

'This does not seem any great matter,' Firenz said slowly. 'After all, this is a task any peasant can accomplish. Your duellists go about the business of a nobleman or soldier, and surely that must be a more complicated task to fashion them for.'

She looked as though she would contradict him directly, which would have been unthinkable, but instead she said, 'It is the greatest achievement of any artificer, my lord, to make a machine that is itself a maker. The dream of every artificer since my craft began is to make a machine so cunningly wrought that it might reproduce itself, but not even the greatest of us has come near to accomplishing such a thing. Our wood-carver could conceivably make each little cog and lever of himself in wood, but he could not put such myriad parts together, alas. It is our sadness, that our little children can never have children of their own.'

Her expression was so mournful that he put a hand to her cheek and she froze, her wide eyes flicking to him, startled as a deer.

'I will not deprive you of your wood-carver,' he told her kindly, 'as you are plainly attached to the industrious old fellow. However, if you have some little manikin that engages in more noble pursuits, tomorrow evening I have some fine friends attending at my townhouse and I would have something special to show them.'

In the end he bought a falconer, whose swung lure was shadowed by a bird of brass that circled and swooped about him, tethered to the metal man by a thread so fine that Firenz could barely perceive it, even knowing it was there. When his peers gathered, he unveiled the little wonder to the amazement of all, and they watched for minute after minute, never seeing bird or lure repeat the same exact motions. At the back, Pauli skulked, disgruntled and displaced. The evening was a grand success.

And yet Firenz was not content. Unhappiness was an affliction that rarely touched his life, and when it did there was always the one same cause: there was something in the world that he desired, and had yet to enjoy.

'Sardos,' he told his servant, 'I am of a mood to return to that artificer's in the Dock Quarter,' as though it was just one of many such places he had visited recently.

He was lazing in his morning room, reclining on a couch in the sunlight that splashed from the tall windows. He had sent for two of the most attractive maids the townhouse had to offer, with the vague idea of honouring the pair of them with his attentions, to take his mind off other things. They were well used to that side of their duties, and presented themselves immaculately, pale and elegant and made-up, necklines cut to show the swell of their breasts, girdles cinched to show the narrowness of their waists. The townhouse's steward knew well his young master's tastes, and a nobleman of Firenz's status should want for nothing, after all.

Now, though, he stared at them listlessly, and found them over-prepared and artificial. A very different manner and complexion was hanging about his mind.

'What value is our patronage there, remind me?'

Sardos gave a figure for the purchase of the falconer, which would have bought a well-trained warhorse or a profitable inn.

'And she seemed grateful, did she not?'

'I am sure she was glad of the coin, lord.'

'That's not what I meant, Sardos. You saw her, she was glad that her little toy had found its way into such discerning, appreciative company. These artificers, more than gold to them is that their cleverness is seen and admired. And to have secured such as I for a client, what a coup for her! Yes, she was duly impressed. I read it in her face.'

Sardos said nothing, but Firenz reviewed his meeting with Amaria and knew it to be true. Besides, he was fully aware of what a fine figure he cut, from his aquiline features and the flawlessly fashionable pallor of his complexion down to his lean swordsman's physique displaying immaculately sculpted calves. No wonder the girl's head had been turned by him. Besides, he was not like Pauli, to jealously guard the source of his new toys. The whole of Leintz would know that the Filigree had his personal approval, and then the girl would not be able to make her little devices fast enough to satisfy demand. That was ever the contract between artisan and a noble of such elevation as Firenz, and such contracts should be properly sealed and concluded.

It was, after all, a matter of entitlement.

The expression on Amaria's face when Firenz pushed his way into the emporium a second time was gratifying. His satisfaction was only a little dented when her questions revolved around the operation of the falconer rather than he himself. Had it functioned correctly? How had his guests reacted? Still, Firenz could turn raconteur when the mood suited him, and so he regaled her with a suitably extravagant telling. She hung on every word as though the success of his diversion was life and death to her, and his words made her so happy that he was struck by a moment of uncharacteristic uncertainty. Seeing that guileless joy there, that her little automaton had impressed, he felt an unfamiliar emotion briefly struggling with his desires. For a second it seemed that he felt a fondness for the girl in a sense that was not proprietary or sexual, and that actually making her happy might have some merit in and of itself. The curious, uncomfortable moment passed.

'I am minded to tell my fellows where such a marvel came from,' he let slip idly, examining the intricacies of a little gilded hart which came with jewelled hounds to chase it. 'You shall not lack for patrons, Amaria.' It was the first time he had addressed her by name, and he relished the feel of it on his tongue.

'My lord is very kind.'

'You are grateful.'

'Exceeding grateful, my lord.' She was at his elbow, reaching for the hart, perhaps to set it in motion to be tracked across the tabletop by its miniature hunters. Before she could touch it, though, he put his hand on hers, feeling the perfect smooth softness of her skin. She had frozen but did not pull away, and surely she had deciphered his meaning and had acquiesced to it. Perhaps it was not the first time her body had become consideration when bartering for custom and patronage. She would know the way of the world as well as Firenz.

'I am of a mind to see your emporium's greatest treasure, Amaria,' he breathed in her ear. Her eyes flicked to him, those exotic features caught between expressions, unreadable.

'My lord?'

'Come now, do not pretend that you don't know the honour of having the son of the Count of Morelle at your door,' he said softly. 'Who else but I, in all the world, can appreciate just how lovely are your wares? I swear, Amaria, that when I stepped into your domain here, the beauty I found quite made a captive of me. You have chained me here, Amaria.'

'I…' Her hand moved again towards the hart but he recaptured it and brought it to his lips. Her eyes, when he met them, were wide with an emotion that he decided was excitement.

'My mother…' she began, voice shaking. By that time Sardos had already moved to the curtain beyond which that hunched figure appeared to slumber. His instructions had been simple: that the old woman would not spoil Firenz's moment with a parent's complaints, if she lacked a commercial mind so much as to make them. In Leintz, most who had a daughter knew that a purse of coin to add to the dowry was worth more than any lost virtue. These artificers were foreigners, though, and hence Sardos had been instructed to be firm.

Firenz had previously spied out another chamber off the shop, and now he encircled Amaria in his arms, pressing her warmth against him, guiding her towards that further room with a nod at Sardos.

'My lord,' said the girl, sounding confused and a little fearful, 'is there some other work you wish demonstrated?'

'Oh, there is,' he confirmed. 'I wish you to show me the most hidden workings of the artificer, for I have seen you take so much pleasure in the demonstration of your art that I know you shall have far more joy showing me the innermost secrets of yourself.'

Sardos watched his master step past the curtain, ears pricked for any motion from the room at his back. There was nothing, and curiosity sparked in him. How oblivious could the lass's mother be to these goings on?

Sardos considered himself a failed man of principle. His home, and his history, had given him a sense of right and wrong and yet, to serve the nobility, such a sense must be laid aside for a while. This current venture was just one more similar business, and he had to comfort himself with the knowledge that the girl would be well rewarded for her time and, after all, what else but that was the primary difference between nobles like Firenz and the lower orders? True emotions – the right to be hurt, offended, outraged - these were noble privileges. For everyone else there was no wrong that sufficient coin could not compensate.

He pushed past the drape and hooked his head around, starting back when he saw her. Yes: there she was, the old woman in her chair, head down as she slept. He was about to draw back, but he had a bodyguard's instincts for the out of place, and he held on, staring. True he saw a human form bundled in heavy black cloth, two withered hands resting on the creased lap, a head nodding over them. Yet there was no motion at all, no rise and fall or whispered murmur to tell of breath. Cat-footed, Sardos crept forwards, frowning.

Three steps in, and he saw the trick of it: that the hands were carefully articulated and pinned at each joint, that the face was a mask, eyes forever closed in wooden slumber.

'Mother' was no more than a puppet, and he grinned at the cleverness of it – the girl had no doubt hoped that the silent presence of this surrogate parent might warn off the very attentions that she was now enduring.

The thought soured his appreciation somewhat, but he had not heard the girl protesting yet, and perhaps that meant she was, despite appearances, one of those who knew how such arrangements worked. If she pleased Firenz, said the right things, made the right noises, then she would profit from it.

Then he heard the scream and his heart sank a little, but only a little. A few years in Firenz's service had rubbed a lot of the shine off his principles.

Firenz could not have asked for better: the room beyond the curtain was Amaria's bedchamber, just as he had imagined it might be. She slept in remarkable luxury there, for the bed had a silk-swaddled pillar at each corner, the canopy merging with the riotous hangings obscuring the ceiling. It was a fit bower for her beauty and his conquest of it, he thought.

'My lord, what do you want?' she whispered. She was trembling very slightly in his grip, and he thought that was a very becoming thing for her to do. With one hand, he turned her chin so that she faced him full on, eyes staring into his with a disarming innocence that suggested the first time would be by far the most revelatory with her – any future liaisons inexpressibly cheapened by the fact that the bloom of her inexperience had gone. He had no doubt, looking now into her half-confused, half-frightened features, that she must be virgin.

'Fear not, I shall treat you as gently as I would one of your delicate devices,' he whispered to her. 'I shall lay open your casement and find the very heart of your workings. I shall tune you and tension you, and then with my key I shall wind you, and all your parts will know true fulfilment.' He had thought some time, on the walk here, over just what terms of endearment were suitable for bedding an artificer. They would make an amusing anecdote when drinking with his fellows later.

'Please,' she whispered, and he took it to mean encouragement, guiding her to the bed and setting her down on it. He let his hands glide from her shoulders to plunge into her gown, forcing it down past her breasts, feeling it resist him a little at first, and then give in to him gracefully, just as it should.

'Mother, please!' she got out, her voice choked. She was tipping towards prudish ingratitude now, shaking beneath him and yet unable to muster the spirit to fight. Instead of this putting him off, abruptly his desire was not to be further frustrated, and he cast her back on the bed with a surprised gasp, ripping down his breeches and hose to spring his member free. He burrowed his hands into her skirts to cast them up, finding her bare thighs and pushing them apart.

She had gone into some peculiar mix of rigidity and limpness, her body fixed in place, yet jerking and swaying with each motion of his. It was not quite the welcoming response he might have hoped for, but the girl would liven up once he was in her, he knew. After all, he was bestowing a great honour on her, and no doubt she would come to appreciate it later, even if not during the act.

His need was ever more pressing, and he had her skirts all rucked up about her waist, his hands stooping on her breasts like hawks even as he thrust himself in between her legs, only to glance painfully off some hard obstruction. He hissed in hurt surprise. Did she have some belt or girdle on, some bar to his manhood that he would have to tussle with? He reached down urgently with one hand, groping at her, each rough movement jerking her entire body. Her hands were poised halfway up towards him, as though arrested in the moment of trying to push him away, swaying every time he fumbled at her, yet never quite completing the rejection.

He found the space between her thighs and scrabbled there for something to strip away or remove. There was nothing. There was nothing at all, no hair, no slit, nothing but smooth skin. She was as featureless as a statue or a doll.

With a horrified inhalation he jerked back from her, but she came with him, without ever losing that weirdly posed looseness of limb. He felt himself enmeshed, caught in a net of strands so fine as to be invisible, and yet too strong for him to free himself from. Every time he moved, she moved like his reflection, arms shaking and swaying as he tried to tug his own limbs free of the unseen strings that he was tangled in.

He stopped, locked in horror, staring at her face that was set, now, in its last fearful expression. Her eyes were unseeing, her mouth partway open. She was perfect and beautiful but, now he saw her, there was nothing of the living woman about her at all.

Then she twitched and moved again, even though he was still, but it was as a marionette jerks when its wires are plucked, nothing living about it. Three times he watched her spasm, and then her eyes focused and she looked up and spoke the word, 'Mother.'

Firenz looked up at what was lowering itself out from the silk-cloaked ceiling, letting itself down those invisible strands limb by limb. His eyes took in the translucent bulk of its body, within which vague shadows moved which might have been alien organs or infinitely delicate mechanisms. He saw its many articulated legs picking their way as it descended upon him. He met its multiple gaze. He saw its fangs spread wide.

It took Sardos a moment too long to realize that the scream, though it had been shrill as a woman's, came from his master's throat. He bolted into the bed chamber, and stopped.

The girl was smoothing her skirts down, standing away from the bed, her hands trembling. Firenz lay on his back on the bed itself, his hose pulled down to mid-thigh, motionless.

Sardos was about to rush to his master's side – yes, and kill the girl, too, if any harm had come to the young lord - but then a voice spoke as the girl straightened up. It was a gentle, firm voice, a woman's voice. It most certainly did not issue from Amaria, or from anyone Sardos could see there in the room.

'I am sorry,' it said. 'I would have acted sooner, my child, but I did not understand his purpose. They are so confusing.'

Amaria's shoulders shook, and she rubbed at her eyes as

though to clear tears or - as Sardos was abruptly certain - to try and make tears come.

'I made you too well,' said that bodiless voice, seeming to come from the very walls. 'You are too near perfect, and the world has no place for perfection, even in our art.'

'Mother,' Amaria whispered. She had not noticed Sardos in the doorway. 'Oh, mother…'

'Please, tell me what I can do to make you well,' said the voice plaintively. 'Let me help you. Let me understand you. Humanity is such a fragile creation, and yet how very complex in its replication. I made you too well, that I cannot fathom your workings now.'

Amaria hugged herself. 'I cannot either,' she said softly.

'We will go elsewhere,' the mother-voice decided. 'I shall find companions for you. Sisters. Brothers. No, I shall make them.' It sounded desperate to please. 'Or perhaps…'

All this time Firenz had been lying motionless on the bed – though Sardos could not have forced himself to go to his master's side for all the gold in the world – but now he moved. In fact he thrust one arm straight up in the air very abruptly, then sat up in a most unnatural way, that hardly seemed to use any muscles a human body might own to. That arm remained stiffly vertical, the hand flopping at the end of it, whilst its opposite limb was completely loose, as was his swaying head.

Sardos wanted very badly to run, then, but he could not tear his eyes away.

'Look!' the mother-voice called gently, and Firenz stood without warning, head still down over his chest. In another sudden transformation he adopted a bizarre posture, one arm still raised, the other hand on his hip, and one leg tucked up so that its foot touched the knee of the other, stretching the lowered hose. His shrunken manhood drooped and danced.

Before Sardos's eyes, Firenz began to execute a slow and careful pirouette, revolving precisely on the spot.

'You see,' said the mother-voice with desperate gaiety, 'he could be a companion for you. Would he amuse you? Would you like that?'

'Mother, no!' Amaria got out, with all the horror that Sardos felt. 'How could you think that would be what I want?'

'I'm sorry, I'm sorry, I don't know how to make you happy,' the despair of any parent whose child is hurt, and who cannot make it better. 'He will be good for parts, though. We can still make use of him. Perhaps you would like to make something of him?'

A look came into Amaria's face such as Sardos had never seen. It had hope in it, though, and a certain ambition, and it made her more beautiful than she had been, whilst at the same time being a look he never wanted to see again.

'Perhaps...' she said, her eyes far away, fixed on some artificer's dream inside her head.

By that time Firenz had finished his flawless pirouette, and when he came to face Sardos again, his head was up and his eyes were open. They locked onto the gaze of his servant and his expression contorted and twitched, shuddering with the need to express himself. 'Help me, please,' came the strangled whisper. 'Sardos, please, help me...'

Amaria's head snapped round to stare at the intruder in the doorway, but by then Sardos was running, and he did not stop running until he had reached the southern city-states of his birth, and ever after he listened out for rumours of a new artificer's emporium in whatever town he lived in and, when he heard of such, he moved on.

Contributors

Paul Weimer

An expat New Yorker who has found himself living in Minnesota for the last 9 years, Paul Weimer has been reading SF and Fantasy for over 30 years and exploring the world of roleplaying games for over 25 years. Almost as long as he has been reading, and watching movies, he has enjoyed telling people what he has thought of them and trying his own hand at writing fiction as well. In addition to his reading, writing, and gaming interests, Paul enjoys taking architectural and landscape photography, with the occasional picture of a SF or Fantasy author who comes to town. Besides his chatty presence on Twitter (@Princejvstin) Paul can be found at his own blog, Blog Jvstin Style, the Functional Nerds, the SF Signal Community, Livejournal and many other places on the Internet.

Alasdair Stuart

Alasdair Stuart is the host of award-winning podcast Pseudopod (www.pseudopod.org) and works as a freelance writer and journalist, specializing in genre fiction in all its forms. Yes, including that one. An enthusiastic amateur baker and martial artist, he's worked for The Guardian, magazines such as Neo, Sci Fi Now and Death Ray and blogs for sfx.co.uk, as well as his own site, www.alasdairstuart.com. His collection of every 2012 Pseudopod essay, The Pseudopod Tapes Volume 1, is also available from Fox Spirit Books.

Fran Terminiello

Francesca Terminiello lives in Surrey with her family and a growing collection of swords. She has previously contributed a short story to the Tales of the Nun & Dragon anthology, also published by Fox Spirit, and is currently putting the finishing touches to her debut novel, a dark and bloody fantasy noir co-written with David Murray.

She spends her spare time contributing to several blogs, as well as practicing and researching Historical European Martial Arts, in particular 16th Century Bolognese swordsmanship and 17th Century Italian rapier.

Fran talks swords at The Girls Guide to the Apocalypse http://www.ggsapocalypse.co.uk and promotes women in Historical European Martial Arts at Esfinges http://esfinges1. wix.com/e. Her own blog can be found at http://franterminiello.wordpress.com/ where she juggles both pen and sword.

C.J. Paget

C.J. hates writing bios. Bios remind him that he's got none of the qualifications to be a science-fiction writer. He doesn't have a PhD in Astro-physics. He wasn't born into a literary or scientific family. He's never worked in interesting fields or places. He wasn't there when major world events went down. He's never lived in far-off places and bathed in the tides of other cultures. He doesn't even own a cat.

He did win the 2011 James White Award. So that's something.

Andrew Reid

Andrew Reid is a writer obsessed with the fantastic and the adventurous. Born in Scotland, he lives in Yorkshire with four chickens, three cats, and an ever-growing stack of unsold novels. You can find him on Twitter as @mygoditsraining, where he will be overjoyed by any mention of movies from the eighties or nineties.

Juliet E McKenna

Juliet E McKenna has always been fascinated by myth and

history, other worlds and other peoples. Her debut novel, The Thief's Gamble, was published in 1999 and 2012 sees the publication of her fifteenth epic fantasy, Defiant Peaks, concluding The Hadrumal Crisis trilogy. She reviews for the web and magazines notably Interzone and Albedo One, teaches creative writing from time to time and fits all this around her husband and teenage sons. She writes diverse shorter fiction from stories for themed anthologies to a handful of tales for Doctor Who, Torchwood and Warhammer 40k, always enjoying the challenge of writing something new and different to her novels.

Rob Haines

Rob Haines is a writer, podcaster and ex-turtle biologist. His work is collected at www.generationminusone.com, and he can be found on Twitter as @Rob_Haines.

Ren Warom

Ren's a writer of the strange, dark and bizarre, not known for an ability to fit into boxes of any description. She's a certified Pirate-nun, mum to three spawn, slave to several cats, writing and editing obsessive and general all round weirdo. The word askance was invented for the way people tend to look at her. Represented by the fabulous Jennifer Udden of Donald Maass Literary Agency, Ren's looking to traumatise a book shop near you very soon. Find her on twitter @RenWarom and on the web at http://renwaromsumwelt.wordpress.com.

Suzanne McLeod

Suzanne McLeod is the author of the Spellcrackers.com urban fantasy series about magic, mayhem and murder – liberally spiced with hot guys, kick-ass chicks and super-cool supes! The Shifting Price of Prey - #4 - is her latest book. Suzanne has been a cocktail waitress, dance group roadie, and retail manager before becoming a writer. She was born in London (her favourite city and home to Spellcrackers.com) and now lives with her husband on the sunny (sometimes) South Coast of England, about a mile away from the sea.

Adrian Tchaikovsky

Adrian Tchaikovsky was born in Lincolnshire, studied and trained in Reading and now lives in Leeds. He is known for the Shadows of the Apt fantasy series starting with Empire in Black and Gold and currently up to Book 8, The Air War. His hobbies include stage-fighting, and tabletop, live and online role-playing. More information and short stories can be found at www.shadowsoftheapt.com.

4371859R00081

Printed in Great Britain
by Amazon.co.uk, Ltd.,
Marston Gate.